Do you want the truth to come out?

to the team
@ TS/CRC
with love,
[illegible]

Bernardo Hinksch

First published in 2023

bearhinksch@gmail.com

To my sister Ana Luiza, who loves books...

Contents

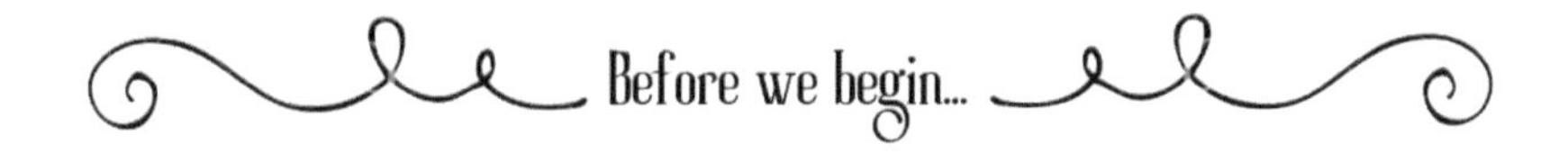

Before we begin...

Dear reader,

I am really thrilled to tell you this story. I would also like to take a moment and pat myself in the back for writing a book. But, before I do all those things, I would like to tell *you* some things.

First, I still don't consider myself a professional author. I write for fun, and this book is another fun project. I always wanted to write a murder mystery, and whodunnits seem to be popular again, so one day I sat down with one small idea in my head and started writing, not knowing how far I would be able to go, or how much that idea would grow. That small idea grew to places I never expected it to, and the result is this book. It was not easy. I knew it wouldn't be, but I didn't imagine it would be *so* difficult. Massive respect for people who write books.

I should also remind you that English is still not my native language, so you might find some spelling and grammatical mistakes here and there. I do apologise for those. A team of good friends read it and looked for mistakes and inconsistencies, but they are also not linguists. In fact, some don't even have English as their first language. They all have a lot of love and dedication, and I love them all for it.

One thing I suspected - and now I'm sure of - is that finding information on the internet about murdering someone and getting away with it is definitely not easy. Probably for a good reason. I also *don't* have a team of assistants, editors or researchers at my disposal, because, and you'll know this already if you didn't skip the first paragraph, I'm not a professional writer. For that reason, you might find things in this book that are not super scientifically accurate to the smallest details - there is some amount of poetic licence here and there. Any feedback will be highly appreciated and welcomed, but please keep this in mind before shouting at me "but this is not how they do it in real life".

I used a lot of people I know as inspiration for my characters, but everyone in this book is fictional and any resemblance with actual persons or facts is purely coincidental. I would also like to make it clear that I never ever did murder anyone and I do not intend to ever murder someone. This is not based on a real story. I mean, it might be a real story for someone in the world, after all we passed 8 billion recently, but not anyone I know. The only thing that reflects reality in this book is Brighton. I did try to get all the references correctly, please feel free to point those that are not. And if you haven't been to Brighton, please come visit. It's a great city.

Another thing about a murder mystery is that it has been done and redone to the square times three. It's very difficult to find an original idea, something that nobody ever did. Some parts of this book might feel like I'm ripping off that novel you once read in high school, but all I did was take inspiration from different stories and people to create my own. If you wrote one of those stories or are one of those people, and feel like I'm using you or your property, please don't sue me. Let's talk about it instead. I don't have the money to pay for lawyers and I am happy to include you as a reference or remove it completely.

I had a great time writing this book, but above all, I had a great time living with these characters. They became part of my life: I woke up thinking about them, slept thinking about them, I dreamed about them. I caught myself having conversations with them, and now that I finished the book, I kind of miss them. I hope you will welcome them into your life too and enjoy their company. I hope you enjoy their story, and I hope you enjoy reading it as much as I enjoyed writing it. If you don't, I'm honestly sorry - but I don't offer a 30 day satisfaction guarantee or your money back kind of deal. Do please let me know why you didn't like it and what I could do better next time. And if you do like it, please leave me a review on Amazon - or wherever you got it.

The last thing I want to tell you is that the killer is... *[insert evil laughter here]*. No, no! I won't make it that easy for you. In fact, I truly hope you don't find out who did it until I tell you. However you find out, please don't tell anyone else. Let them also try and figure it out - if they can.

Finally, thank you very much for purchasing this book. Your support means a lot.

Good hunting.

Bernardo

Chapter One

Anywhere but Brighton

It was a cold and sunny Monday morning in January, the second day of the year, when I first entered the place where I would work for the next six months: Brighton's police station. Our graduation ceremony took place some twenty days prior, but the holidays made it feel like it was another lifetime altogether.

As I walked through the door of the police station, I thought about our final day at the academy, and the moment we were receiving our posting letters sprang to my mind. Up until that point, we had been training for the previous six months to become private investigators, and it had not been easy on any of us. We somehow formed a strong bond, and we were all very excited to see where life would take us next, who would be there with us, what we would do. After six months of books, lectures, videos and tests, we all wanted to get out of the classroom and get into the action.

I remember all those things going through my mind the day I opened my letter, and how the words came out of my mouth before I could hold them. Before I could think about them, even.

"You gotta be kidding me!"

My classmates all turned around, almost as if they had rehearsed and synchronised the movement. Some of them were grinning, some seemed genuinely worried. One thing was sure: I managed to break the tension in the classroom.

The next module of training would be a paid placement internship in some sort of related workplace, and throughout the training we were able to manifest our preference for the kind of crimes we would like to investigate. Some people wanted to go into fraud and financial crimes, some wanted to go into cyber crimes. I wanted to go into police investigation - I grew up reading the likes of Poirot and watching Murder She Wrote on TV, it was clear to me that I wanted to be a detective. Maybe for that very reason, I applied to do my internship at Sussex Police. I did not *really* want to be a member of the police, but that would probably be the closest I would get from actual police work. I also told my colleagues I was hoping to be posted in a small, quaint village in the middle of nowhere, preferably the home of some kind of rich person living in a huge manor, who would later be killed by a diamond encrusted dagger in the library. My main suspect would be a mysterious woman with a strong exotic accent. I was obviously making a joke - although, as the cliche goes, every joke has a grain of truth to it.

As much as I wanted to be involved in investigations and be part of the action, there was a side of me that wanted to live in a small and peaceful place, where there would be practically no violence, and I would be able to help the community. I didn't care which small village I would be deployed to, whether there would be any action or not, as long as I did not end up in the biggest city in Sussex: Brighton and Hove. 'Anywhere but Brighton' became my mantra. As luck would have it, those were the exact two words written in my posting letter.

It was not really a surprise, to be fair. The vast majority of investigations and police work took place in big cities, where things actually happen. Places like Brighton, Eastbourne, Worthing. A lot also happened in Gatwick, but it was a different kind of work which I was not really interested in. Only a small handful of people worked at the villages, and there was not really space or need for interns. Sadly, I was not the exception.

I wouldn't have been that upset with any other big city, but the thought of living in Brighton scared me. Mainly because it brought with it the prospect of dealing with drunk young people, tourists, misogynists and homophobes. In a nutshell, I was not happy with what that letter and, to some extent, life had given me. My interjection just showed that clearly to my colleagues.

At least this would be a six month experience placement, and after that I would have the chance to move somewhere else, with undeniably good experience on my CV. So I put on a brave face and decided to play with the cards I had been dealt. I decided to try and make the best of it. Whether I would succeed or not, was a completely different matter. But more on that later.

It had not been that difficult to find accommodation - who would not want to rent to someone working with the police, especially as we were now being paid for our work? I got myself a small one bedroom flat in Hanover, about a ten minutes walk from the police station on John Street. I didn't have many things, so I made sure to rent a place which was already furnished. It did not feel very homely and personal to me, but neither did the idea of a life in Brighton - at least there was a consistent theme.

That first day was purely focused on admin work: taking pictures for my ID, setting up my email address and access to systems, documents, learning to use the equipment and the programs. Most of the theory we had already learned in the academy, now it was just a matter of putting it into practice. I was also introduced to the people who, unbeknownst to me at the time, would be who I would work most closely towards the following months: Lead Detective Stephen Pritchard and Senior Forensic Analyst Dr Sanjay Parkheet.

Steve, as he asked me to call him, was a tall man in his mid forties, with thick brown hair, that didn't seem to have been cut by an actual profession in a good number of years, thick connecting brows, over piercing blue eyes. His face also showed a stubble from someone who hadn't shaved for the last couple of days, although I couldn't say if he achieved this look intentionally or if he just didn't care. He was not attractive, but he was also not ugly. He was the kind of man people don't really notice - he looked like a common person, and there was nothing special or outstanding about him. For him, it would have been very easy to blend in, as long as he kept his mouth shut: he had an unmistakably strong accent from the North of England which, in Brighton, would be something that would make someone stand out from the crowd. He had been working for the police for the last twenty something years, and he gave me the impression he was someone who was once very good, but got lost within the system.

Dr Sanjay was the exact opposite: he was young, probably around twenty-eight years old, always very well dressed and well groomed. His neatly combed brown hair was never seen without hair gel, his eyes were honey brown, he was clean shaven and some people said never left the house without cologne. He graduated top of his class at Cambridge and repeated to whoever wanted to hear that forensics was his dream job, and the solution was always in the details the eyes cannot see. He had married his best friend from childhood, Pryia, and already told me how they lived across from each other their whole lives, and how he knew she would be his wife from the very first time they met. She was about six months pregnant and they were having trouble choosing a name for the newborn - the first fight they've ever had about anything.

The team was supported by Ms Felicity Browne-Porter, who insisted everyone call her Felicity. She was in her early to mid sixties, grey hair that contrasted with her dark skin tone, thick turtle shell glasses with equally thick lenses and a maternal face that reminded me of a kind grandma. She often said her own grandchildren didn't see her with such kind eyes, and she always called everyone 'darling'. Her husband had passed away some four or five years prior, leaving her a considerable sum of inheritance. She has been in the system for many years, working for different government agencies, and said that, without work, she would go insane. On the other hand, she kept a calendar counting the years left until she would retire in Spain. She made sure to mention that she considered herself an enemy of the Conservative Party and was probably the person who made me feel most welcomed in the new job.

Besides them, I was also introduced to many other people working that day, from janitors to heads of departments, but I could not keep everyones' names in my mind. It was a long and busy day, but at the same time nothing really interesting happened. Well, apart from the occasional gossipy comment from Felicity about the things that happened at the office Christmas party some weeks prior. They could not shock me, because I did not know any of the people who took part in any of the stories described by her, but some of my colleagues seemed to be a bit uncomfortable with this. Others thought it funny and harmless. One of my colleagues told me, discreetly, while Felicity was out of the room:

“Forget the BBC News, if you want to be up to date with anything that happens around here, tune into FBP News.”

At least with the busy day I didn't notice the time passing, and I was surprised when the clock showed five minutes past six in the afternoon. I gathered my things and left the building, but went in the opposite direction of my new place, as I needed to do some grocery shopping. I noticed Steve outside, by the edge of the building, having a cigarette. I stopped for a chat.

“Welcome to the team, kid. Did you like your first day?”

“To be fair, it was a lot of admin and boring things. Which is normal, I guess. But I cannot wait for the action to start.”

“Action? What do you mean?”

“I don’t know, the real investigations, the gruesome murders...”

“That’s interesting. So you *want* people to be murdered?”

That question caught me off guard. After six months in the classroom and being so eager to start working, it became easy for me to disassociate the fact that every time a crime is committed, someone becomes a victim. Someone real, with a life and feelings, with loved ones and a history. Steve seemed to have picked up on what I was thinking.

“This is the first thing you need to learn about working with the police: a victim is not a number. A victim is a person, and they should always be treated as such. Even your suspects, they are also real human beings. Don’t ever forget that.”

I felt a little embarrassed, especially as he had a somewhat condescending tone, maybe with an undertone of kindness. Sounded like someone who didn't want to show vulnerability, as if he had to assert there and then who was the boss and what my place was. Seeing me clearly embarrassed and uncomfortable, he went on, this time a little less condescendingly.

“Hey, don’t beat yourself up. It’s not the first time you will get yourself thinking like that. Happens to everyone, you're not the first one I’ve had to give this advice to. I still have to remind myself sometimes, after these many years. In any case, keep your expectations low. There are a lot of small crimes in Brighton, but I would be very surprised if you got any 'action' in your six months here. You will probably end up helping many departments. And it's probably better this way: to be here and not be used, it means the world is a safer place. Don't you agree?"

I was not sure I could read him yet, or if I would ever be able to. All I knew was that day one was over, now it was time to get some food and get away from the cold, to enjoy my new home.

Yet, somehow I had the clear impression things did not start well for me.

Chapter Two

When you least expect it...

For a moment I thought I was still standing in the corner of the building, chatting to Steve while he finished his cigarette.

"Hey kid, get up. We need to move."

The words from him came into my head whilst I realised I was in my bed, but at this point I still could not discern if those words were reality or part of the dream I was having, which I could not remember anymore. I think my phone had been ringing for what seemed like hours, and I had no idea of the time. Slowly, my brain started to recall what happened the night before. I stopped at the shop to get some food - ready-made curry for one, which I heated in the microwave with a surprisingly tasty garlic and coriander naan on the side - sat in front of the TV to watch some reruns of Schitts Creek, and it wasn't long until I was sleeping and drooling. How I made it to my bed is a mystery not even Miss Marple would have been able to solve.

I finally opened my eyes, looked at my side clock - it was showing three fifty two AM. I somehow managed to get myself together and say something, in a very raspy voice.

“Hello, Steve. I think I am awake. What is going on?”

“Something happened. We are coming to pick you up, can you be ready in fifteen?”

“Fifteen what? *Minutes?* Wow, let me think. I need to shower, eat something...”

“Don’t worry about food, we will get something on our way. Shall we say ten past?”

“Can we make it a quarter past, at least?”

“Ok, I will see you then. I hope you’re ready to put your money where your mouth is.”

At a quarter past four I was closing the building door behind me when I saw the faint blue/red light reflection from the car entering the street. When they stopped, I could see that Steve was driving and Dr Sanjay was sitting in the back seat. That early hour seemed to have enhanced the first impression I had of them both: Steve looked even rougher than usual, whilst Dr Sanjay looked even better groomed than when we first met.

Once on our way, they filled me in on the reason we were out so early: Someone had been found dead at a flat in the Marina area of town, but we did not yet have many details. We were informed that the victim appeared to be an adult male, found by a neighbour who was coming back from a night out; he lived on the third floor, which was also the top floor. The witness had been out the whole of the previous day with friends. When she came home, she noticed that the victim's flat door was slightly ajar, and tried to alert him about it. She called for the victim and there was no answer. Consequently, she went further inside and found the victim, laying face down on the couch, unresponsive. The witness did not touch anything and called the police right away.

The call was received by the emergency services at eighteen past three AM, and the police arrived about fifteen minutes later. It was clear to the first responders that the victim had been dead for many hours, no CPR was administered and he was pronounced dead at forty five minutes past three AM. The officer in charge of the scene alerted Steve, who immediately called Dr Sanjay and me. At the moment, the death was being treated as 'under suspicious circumstances', but it was not possible to say anything else until we investigated further. On our way, we would be stopping at a fast food restaurant for a quick breakfast before proceeding to the scene of the crime. And Steve seemed to be even more condescending in the early hours of the morning.

"Oi, mind what you eat! A dead body can be pretty gruesome, especially if it's the first time you see one."

"I mean, we have studied *many* crime scenes in the academy, pictures, videos..."

"Yeah, but this is real life. Trust me, don't order anything with eggs. We can't afford to deal with you being a liability today."

I felt somewhat unwanted there, and resigned myself to a cup of coffee, some fruits and an unappealing though warm muffin sandwich with a slice of cheese in between, which I devoured on the way between the restaurant and the victims' flat. Right in front of the building, there was one other police car, the paramedics ambulance, some police officers and paramedics. A couple of neighbours were out, but the scene was still relatively quiet.

We climbed the stairs and arrived at the flat, where a police officer was standing in front of it, whilst another one was inside the witness' flat opposite, talking to her. We were informed that her name was Alisson Ling, and she seemed a bit ecstatic by the situation. Steve and Dr Sanjay wanted to look at the scene of the crime before talking to her.

The flat was a standard two bedroom, two bathroom flat. We entered through a small corridor that had five doors connecting to further rooms: the first door to the left was a kitchen, the next one clockwise was a small office, right in front of us was a toilet, right beside it to the right was the entrance to the living room, and finishing the circle was the door to the master bedroom. It was not difficult to spot the body after only a few steps into this corridor, as the curtains of the balcony door were open and the light from outside was illuminating the living room. I also noticed a glass on the floor and a stain on the carpet, which was probably the liquid that spilled from the glass as it was dropped. My first thought was that the body could have easily been spotted from outside too, but once I stood at the door, I saw why I was wrong: between the balcony door and the couch stood a bookshelf filled with books, blu-ray discs, records and board games. Light could still go through, but the view would be blocked enough not to allow any outside looker to see it clearly. And as we were on the top floor, not many other buildings had a good point of view into the flat.

I was lost in my initial analysis when I saw Steve's hand stopping me, almost hitting me in the face.

“Sorry, kid. That's as far as you'll go for now.”

“Are you kidding me? *You won't allow me in the crime scene?*”

“No, I will not. This is no place for amateurs. Everything we find now will be extremely important to the investigation, and I cannot allow you to contaminate or compromise it in any way.”

Before I could protest, he made his point clear.

“This is not a game, it's not a classroom. This is real life. You should be happy I'm allowing you all the way up here. You’re just an intern. Observe from the door if you want. And if you don't, go back to bed. I don't care, I have a death to investigate.”

I was extremely frustrated but there was nothing I could do, so I decided to make the best of the situation and observe.

Dr Sanjay seemed to be very technical about it all, observing and making annotations. He would move things with surgical precision, making sure that it went back to the exact same place. He seemed to observe everything without making any remarks or change of expression. I felt like he was the kind of person who would not get to a conclusion without knowing all the facts. Steve, on the other hand, gave me a completely different impression. He did not really touch anything, but he would look at things and whisper, whistle, make interjections and ask himself things like "how is it possible", to almost immediately answer with "ah, of course" within the same breath. Maybe I was starting to resent Steve, and that was influencing my judgement, but more and more he looked like a fraud to me.

About half an hour later, after they finished with their observations, we moved to the adjacent flat to talk to Alisson, whilst the forensic team came in to collect objects and take pictures. The body would be removed later.

Now, in the neighbouring flat, I was allowed to come in with them, but I was nudged not to talk, just observe.

Alisson Ling was tall, did not look older than twenty-two, maybe twenty-three years old, and spoke very fast in a very thick accent. She looked east asian, her hair was short, very straight and black with highlights; her eyes were green, although I could have sworn she wore coloured contact lenses, and her mouth was small, which contrasted with her round face. She wore a pink t-shirt with the words 'Girls just wanna have fun' written in gold glittery detail. She now looked tired and extremely fed up with the situation she found herself in - the excitement had certainly passed.

“This is very surreal, d'ya know what I'm sayin'? I come ‘ome after a day out with m'mates and I find a bloody corpse!”

I thought to myself ‘Well not quite, I couldn’t see any blood’, but decided it was wiser to remain silent. She went on.

“I din't even know this bloke. Seen ‘im a couple o’times passing, but never even spoke a word to ‘im. Saw the door a bit open, thought to myself: might've gone to bed after a couple o’pints and forgot to lock the door, bloody idiot. I went in, called 'hullo matey’, no answer, walked a bit in and saw it. Right 'ere where I live, man. It's mad! D'you know what I mean? Mad.”

Steve was the one who spoke to her, and his tone sounded much kinder to her than it ever did to me.

“Miss Ling, we will need you to come down to the police station and make a statement.”

“Oh, call me Ali, Mrs Ling is me mum. D’ya think I can get some sleep first? I'm knackered, d'ya know what I...”

"I understand, Ali. But it's important that this is done now, in the heat of the moment. Otherwise you might forget something, some detail."

"Mate, I don't think I can ever forget this. Anyway, I told yous everything. There's not much more."

"Then it will be a quick statement and you'll be able to get back home and sleep in peace, knowing you fulfilled your duty as a good citizen. We promise we won't keep you for long, and I will make sure someone drives you back home straight away."

Having nothing else there for us, we drove back to the station. Ali came with us in the car, gave her statement and was taken back home. Indeed her statement did not add much more to what she told us, she was just able to clarify details such as times, where she was and who she had been with, and if she would be willing to help further if needed.

In her statement she said that she had left her flat a little after noon, she was pretty sure that the victim's door was closed, but she did not really look. She went to a friend's house in Portslade with two other friends and stayed there the whole afternoon - all of them would be able to vouch for her - and the four of them went to get some food and drinks in the evening. She left those friends around two thirty AM and took the night bus home. She had a cigarette downstairs before going up. When she reached the third floor, as she had to pass in front of the victim's front door to reach her own, she noticed the door ajar. She went in, called for someone, did not get any answer and went further in. That was when she saw the body. She tried to get a response and noticed that the body was cold and rigid, so she called the emergency number right away.

She did not know the victim very well, couldn't even tell what the victim's name was, and had never engaged in any meaningful conversation with the victim, apart from the occasional greeting whilst crossing each other in the common areas of the building. She made herself available for any further clarifications, although insisting there was nothing more to be said, confirmed her contact details and signed her statement after reading it.

After she left, Steve seemed to be back to his usual bad mood.

"Fucking humans. Someone had been found dead, a life was lost, and all she cared about was getting some sleep first. Selfish prick."

"You didn't seem to be so angry at her when she was around."

"Alright Sherlock, what would you rather have me do? Let's hear *your* great idea! Antagonise and spook a key witness into keeping her mouth shut? Brilliant, why didn't I think of that."

I felt like he got me once again, but I was not going to show it.

"Whatever. I'm gonna get some coffee, real coffee, do you want something?"

"Nah, thanks."

I left the building and walked to a cafe a block away, to get some coffee but also to clear my head and take a break from everything. It had been an intense morning, and I finally got what I had so joyfully joked about for the past six months: a murder, a crime scene, investigations, witnesses. But I wasn't sure I actually wanted any of that anymore. It was not exactly how I expected it to go. My whole experience in Brighton so far was not exactly what I thought it would be - if anything, it was worse.

The previous words from Steve echoed in my mind: a life had been lost. I hated to agree with him about anything. Furthermore, this was only day two, and I still had six more months ahead of me. I walked slowly back to the police station, because I did not really want to go back there, but I also wasn't sure if I wanted to go back into that life, that situation that somehow I got myself into. My body was taking the steps back, but my mind was wandering aimlessly, while I looked vaguely ahead of me. When I entered the police station, my mind was suddenly brought back to reality by the person I saw sitting at the reception area. If she was trying to be inconspicuous, she had failed miserably.

She was wearing a pin striped purple suit and trousers and a floral scarf tied around her neck, which immediately made me think of a flight attendant's uniform, accompanied by thick squared indigo blue glasses but almost no make up. Her shoes somehow clashed with the outfit: she wore black converse with pink details; it was not an unpleasant combination, just the type of pairing one wouldn't expect to work. But it did work on her.

Her eyes were grey and hair was somewhere between blond, grey and white, short and ruffled, as if she had left it wet from the shower and shook her head vigorously to try and dry it. She was in her late forties, maybe early fifties, and although I couldn't really tell how tall she was while she was sitting, I would have guessed she was an average height - didn't seem too tall or too short. A small badge on the left side of her chest showed the words 'she/her'.

Felicity came out to talk to her, and I had the impression I was seeing two distant cousins together - although they did not look anything like each other physically. There was something in their manner that looked like they were very familiar with one other. They were walking in the same direction as me, and we entered the room together. As we did, Steve rolled his eyes at the sight of the three of us and said, in an exasperated tone:

"Now this is all that I need, the *famous* Helga Hildegard. To what do we owe the pleasure of having a world renowned detective in our humble investigation?"

Chapter Three

...the unexpected happens

"First of all, mate, it's *Mrs* Hildegard. But I guess manners would be too much to expect from you. Secondly, if I wanted sarcasm, I would be talking to my wife - who can actually do it well - but certainly not to you, Detective Pritchard."

"Seriously, woman! You used to have a better sense of humour. I'm sorry, *Mrs* Hildegard. And you know you can call me Steve."

"Ah, are we doing first names? Alright, you can call me *Mrs Hildegard*, Detective Pritchard."

So that was Helga Hildegard! Up until this point, I had no idea I was in the presence of one of the most famous and respected detectives in England. We studied many of her cases in the academy, when she seemed to have found the solution where everyone else had stumbled. She had very peculiar methods that were unusual but entirely legitimate. Most importantly, she always abided by the law and played fairly. Needless to say, I was fascinated by that woman. In less than ten seconds she went from someone I didn't know, to someone I heard about, someone who caused an impression on me, and finally my new personal hero. She went on.

"To answer your question, I am here on behalf of Mr Honeywell."

"Mr Honeywell?"

"Mr Jack Honeywell was found murdered this morning by the police. Or do you still not know who your victim is?"

Steve looked dumbfounded, but he quickly composed himself. He would not give up that easily.

"That information is confidential to the police, so I won't be able to confirm or deny anything at this point."

"Very well, do as you please - it doesn't matter anyway."

"We are treating the case as 'death under suspicious circumstances' - what makes you think he was murdered?"

"Mr Jack Honeywell came to my office yesterday afternoon while I was out and insisted with the receptionist to speak to me. Unfortunately I couldn't make it back in time, and he left before I arrived. Miss Hughes told me that he said he wished to talk to me urgently, as he feared his life was in danger."

"Very interesting, indeed! And you, as a good citizen, came to the police with that information. Well done! We thank you very much."

"*I am not finished.*"

She spoke the words with a slight, almost imperceptible pause between them. Her tone was strong but not intimidating. It was clear she knew how to command a room. She continued.

"This morning I got a call from the actual Mr Honeywell I am representing: Andrew, a cousin that lives in Essex, not very far from London. Andrew is not exactly the next of Kin, but he was - how can I put it - *thrown* into this position by recent events, as I'm sure you're all well aware."

I was so taken by her theatrical manner that I didn't really think much about the name, until that last statement suddenly hit me. Lord James Honeywell, Esq had been one of the most prolific and controversial barristers in the country. His company, Honeywell-Dupont, made its name, and with it, a vast fortune, by defending those considered indefensible. They were behind the most difficult and, I should add, popular cases, always advocating in a position that went against public opinion. If someone did something very bad, their hope would be for it to attract enough publicity and get a call from Honeywell-Dupont's team. They chose their clients, and reached out to them to be their defendant. They would win about half the cases, but their reputation was built on the fact that they would look for such cases. And even when they couldn't win, they would get their clients deals that were considered impossible. He had a partner, Mr Cedric Dupont, Esq, considered a sidekick. Mr Dupont was European, I think French or Belgian, and he did not attract as much attention as Lord Honeywell.

The truth is that Lord Honewell was the real star in the team. The press hated him, and he was always the subject of speculation in tabloids. But nothing was ever officially confirmed, as he was a very reserved man. He did not give many interviews, and whenever he did, was with the sole purpose of discussing his cases. He would often say that everyone deserves the right to a competent defence and a fair trial.

In the beginning of the previous year Lady Sarah Honeywell, his longtime wife, passed away suddenly following an unfortunate skiing accident in the Italian Alps, and the tabloids couldn't get enough of it. Lord Honeywell announced shortly thereafter that he was retiring with immediate effect to spend time with his children. He only had a son, named Jack, but also raised his nephew Andrew, who became an orphan when he was two years old and was taken in by Lord and Lady Honeywell. Some tabloids speculated that his relationship with his sons was strained, and his retirement was a way to mend it. Others said Jack and Andrew were like brothers, while many insisted

Andrew was never treated as well as Jack. Both of them tried to be out of the spotlight, and lived normal lives.

Not long after all that, Lord Honeywell's name went back into the papers when he was diagnosed with terminal pancreatic cancer and moved to his home in Hove to be closer to the sea. He was a man in his early sixties, and many op eds suggested that his ailments and his certain death whilst still relatively young were the result of karma, due to his professional choices in life.

The whole crime suddenly became much more interesting in my eyes. Steve remained unimpressed.

"Alright, so the nephew called you. And how does that concern me?"

"Andrew would like me to join the investigation team, because he also thinks there's foul play involved. In fact, he is on his way here now, but I wanted to give you a heads up, as a professional courtesy."

"And since when do I have to take orders from *Andrew*?"

He spoke with a disdain that was only trampled by the face of someone who thought they had played their final card. At that moment, my whole time in the academy and in Brighton flashed before my eyes. I was about to see the person who suddenly made me feel confident and comfortable go away for good, and my mouth started speaking before I could think.

"Well, you don't *have* to take orders from anyone. But isn't it your job to find out who is involved in this death and arrest them? Maybe you are forgetting that! Here you have one of the best detectives in the country offering her help, and out of pure spite you will probably refuse it. What's wrong with you? She's not the enemy."

As soon as the last word came out of my mouth, I knew that I had crossed the line. Steve looked like he was about to grab me around my neck and strangle me. Felicity had a discreet grin on her face. Mrs Hildegard looked at me curiously, but I was not sure if she had welcomed this passionate defence from my side. Nobody spoke for a while, and I lowered my head and kept looking at the ground. The next voice who spoke was not familiar, which made me instinctively look up.

"Your colleague raises an interesting point."

Then, almost as if regretting saying something, the new voice continued, with less assurance.

"Sorry, I didn't mean to eavesdrop, but I kind of agree. I just arrived in town and came straight over here. My name is Andrew, erm... Andrew Honeywell."

Andrew was clearly related to his uncle. He was probably approaching his thirties. His hair was a shade darker than strawberry blond, with beard and eyebrows matching the colour. His eyes were leafy green, and his face was dotted by very discreet freckles. He was a bit taller than us all, and I would probably have guessed his height passed the sixt feet mark. His voice was soft and his tone was almost apologetic, apart from his first statement. We did not know it yet, but that tendency of saying the first thing that popped into his head was something very characteristic of Andrew. I could definitely relate!

Mrs Hildegar was the next person who spoke. She did not talk to Andrew, but addressed me instead.

"You must be the new intern."

Her eyes shone with curiosity, and I could practically see the wheels turning inside her head through them.

"You seem clever. I wonder what kind of horrible thing you did in a past life to end up working here, with the likes of the great detective Pritchard. Well, it doesn't matter. You are welcome to join me in my investigation - that is, of course, if the detective does not object to it?"

Steve spoke, and his voice still had a hint of defiance to it, although it also felt like he was running out of options.

"I will have to think about it - having a civilian in the investigation and releasing my intern, it's not so simple as just waltzing into a police station and asking."

"Come on, my good detective. You know these people are lawyers, they're well connected... I will ultimately get what I want. Besides, all I am asking is to be a part of it. To join the investigations, be part of the briefings, and maybe ask a question or two sometimes. But mostly, I will be in the background, you will probably not even notice me here."

Everyone there chuckled, because it was clear that this would not be the case.

"As your intern very cleverly observed earlier, I am not the enemy. I am here to help. As a matter of fact, I already instructed Miss Hughes, the receptionist in my office's building, to come in during her lunch break to give you a statement. I also took the liberty to ask the building management to provide the police with a copy of the CCTV footage from yesterday, which will show you the visit from the victim."

Steve finally looked defeated, as if he had reached the end of his arguments.

"Alright, damn it. You can join, but as a consulting part. Everything goes through me. Is that clear?"

"Perfectly clear, detective. Thank you very much for your kindness - I assure you, you won't regret it. Now we must be going, we have a lot to do. For starters, I would like to take a look at the scene. I assume the police are done with their forensic work, photographing everything, collecting all the clues..."

"Yes, the scene is all yours. But don't mess with it."

"You know me well enough not to be asking me this, detective. Felicity, always a pleasure! What about you, mate, are you coming?"

She was asking me. I was surprised by it, as I did not think her invitation earlier to be serious. But here was my chance to do some actual investigation with someone I could actually enjoy working with. I turned to Steve and asked if he was ok with it.

"I don't give a damn."

I took that as a yes, with a smile on my face.

Chapter Four

Do you want the truth to come out?

The three of us left together - Hildegard, Andrew and me. When we reached the street, she invited Andrew and me for a cup of coffee. But we did not go into the cafe by the police station, we walked a little further into Kemptown until we found a quirky little place called Diva. The owner was a lovely, loud and effusive woman, who greeted us all with 'my loves' in a thick european accent, despite never meeting Andrew or myself. She did seem to know the investigator well, and I could totally picture them being best friends. We ordered our drinks and sat down. As soon as we had our first sips, Hildegard started addressing Andrew. Her tone was serious, in a way I haven't yet heard. She spoke clearly and concisely, as if this was a speech she had already rehearsed.

"Mr Honeywell, the reason I wanted to talk to you here, in private, away from all the eyes of the police, is to ask you something important. I need you to listen to me until the end, don't rush into answering with the first thing that pops into your head. Can you do that?"

"Yes. And please, call me Andrew. Mr Honeywell feels very formal."

"Ok, Andrew. My question is quite simple: Do you want the truth to come out?"

She paused, probably for a dramatic effect. It seemed to have worked, because the question had taken both of us by surprise - we looked equally astonished by it. She continued, still very serious, putting the emphasis on certain words.

"You see, you hired me to investigate this matter, but as soon as I start my investigation, I will not work for *you* anymore, I will work for *the victim*. I will work *for the truth*. Once I start, there is no stopping it, I will go until the truth is found, no matter who it affects. Therefore, as the person hiring me, I am giving you the choice to stop this *now*. If you want to change your mind, *this is the time*. Say the word and I will exit the case and leave all the work to the police."

We all remained silent for a couple of minutes, and the investigator started speaking again. Her tone was now kinder, although still serious.

"Please don't read anything into this question. I am not singling you out. This is a question I ask all my clients before I start a case. Over the years, I have learned not to emotionally involve myself with a case. If you don't want me to proceed, I will leave this case entirely to the police and mind my own business somewhere else. But if you do, it will become my duty to find out the truth, regardless of the outcome and who it affects. So, I will ask you again: do you want the truth to come out?"

Andrew tried to put himself together and answered as convincingly as he could. He seemed very nervous to be put on the spot like that, which probably reflected in his choice of words.

"Yes, I want you to be part of this investigation. If that means discovering the truth, so be it."

That seemed to be good enough for Hildegard.

"Very well. We must lose no time then. I believe you have yet to formally identify the body? I want to be present for that. I also hope to get news from detective Pritchard about a briefing this afternoon. I expect you to be part of this briefing, so we will probably see you later. Now, go get some rest, have something to eat. You look awful, mate."

That last remark came out in a motherly tone, and I am sure Andrew took it that way. Hildegard paid for the drinks and we thanked the Cafe owner, who once again addressed us as if we were her longtime friends. I would definitely come back here at some point.

As we left the Cafe, we crossed the street and stood at the bus stop, waiting for the number seven bus, which would take us to the Marina. The next bus would come in about nine minutes, and that gave me time to properly introduce myself to Hildegard. I finished by asking how she heard about me.

"My business is to know things. Do you think the top of the class would come for an internship at Sussex police and I would know nothing about it?"

"Wow, you're good! How could you possibly know I was top of my class?"

"I didn't, mate. You just confirmed my suspicions."

I couldn't hide my smile. She smiled back.

"I am glad to see you smile. You looked really bad the first time I saw you, while I was sitting at the station, and I guess it was more than having been up since four AM?"

"It has not been easy to work with Steve."

"I suspected. He is a peculiar man, Steve Pritchard. He is not a mean person per se, he is just incompetent and dumb. I remember when he started at the police, he was an intern, just like you. But he was charming and knew how to sell himself."

The idea of Steve being charming was not something that crossed my mind in the slightest. She was quick to read me.

"Yes, as far-fetched as that can be, he was once a charming young man. He could charm anyone on his path, which helped him climb the ladder through the system. Until the time he came to work in my team."

"Were you in the police?"

"Oh yes, I was lead investigator - the same post he occupies today. And being in the team of the best investigators in the country was very beneficial for him. He had the charm and the experience to get any job he would like, anywhere in the country. But he wanted *my* job. He could not accept that I was better than him. I knew that he was not very bright, but he was a hard worker, and his ability to talk to people was very useful to the team. We were a good bunch. When I decided to leave, he was the natural first choice. I was against it, because I did not think he was able to pull it off. He was not a good leader, and his talents would have been better used helping someone else who was actually competent. But once again he managed to charm his way through. And, as I predicted, he could not do the job. He knows that, and that broke something on him. He let himself go. You know when you see a dog chasing a car? Have you ever wondered what the dog would do when he reached the car? He is the dog, he reached the car, but he doesn't know what to do with it. He also hates the idea that he did not beat me, as I only got better after I left."

"Why did you leave?"

"That's a story for another day. Here comes the bus."

About twenty minutes later we were entering the flat. The officer guarding the door had already been advised of our visit. I walked immediately toward the living room, but once again I was stopped from entering it - this time by Hildegard, who told me that it would be the last place we would see. We put on gloves and went into the kitchen first. It was clean and neat, the dishwasher was empty and there was nothing on top of the hob, inside the oven, no dishes in the sink or the rack. There were clothes inside the washing machine that seemed to have been washed but not taken out. Hildegard opened the door and we could smell wet clothes that had been left there for a while. She looked through them, and closed the machine door after. The fridge content did not show anything outstanding, apart from what you'd expect from a young person's fridge.

We went into the office next. It had a bookshelf filled with books and some other small things, and on the opposite side there was an office table/chair set with a laptop on top. The laptop was open but seemed to be off. Hildegard tried to turn it on, but it seemed that its battery was depleted. A board hung on the wall above the laptop, and there were some letters attached to it - a notice from the Marina management, a dentist appointment, a Christmas card.

There were also some pictures - for the first time I could see the victim clearly, and I only recognised him due to his resemblance to Andrew. It was clear they were cousins. They had the same hair colour, same shade of beard, different haircuts. Jack's eyes were a deep brown, and his cheeks looked a bit chubbier than Andrew's, but the light freckles were also present, maybe a bit more prominent in Jack. There was also a picture of what surely was his parents. He had inherited his looks from his father, the resemblance was uncanny, but his eyes came from his mom. The three of them looked happy together, as often it can be seen in family portraits. Andrew was not in the picture, but right beside it was a similar picture of the family, this time with Andrew. Someone who did not know them would have easily guessed they were related, maybe even brothers, although, for a good observer, Andrew's eyes were not the same as Lady Sarah's.

There was also one more picture that seemed to have been taken recently: a group of six people in something that looked like a christmas party. Amongst them Andrew and Jack, each on an opposite side. From left to right first stood Jack, beside him a woman who tried to hug him, but he did not hug her back. She was looking at another woman, who was standing to her right, with a look of disdain. That second woman was hugging a man, who looked like a construction worker who had a quick shower before coming to a party he had not been invited to. Right beside that man stood another man, this one clearly older than everyone else. I had a feeling I had seen him before, but I couldn't remember where from. And beside him, at the right end of the picture, stood Andrew.

Besides Jack, Andrew and the man I thought I recognised, I did not know who those other three people were, I had never seen any of them before.

The next door was a toilet that connected the office to the main corridor. That toilet appeared not to have been used in a while. It was not dirty, but there was a small layer of dust above its surface. I would not have been surprised to find out nobody used it in a week or so. It had nothing out of the ordinary, nothing we would not have expected in a toilet: hand towel and hand soap around the sink area, a bucket under the sink with cleaning products, bath bubbles, a bath bomb, a bottle of shower gel and a bottle of shampoo in the far corner of the shower/bathtub... Nothing seemed unusual with it, therefore this was the room we spent the least amount of time in.

The next room was the living room, but we skipped that door and went into the master bedroom. It had a small corridor that opened into a bedroom area with a small en-suite bathroom to the right. This bathroom showed signs of being used - again, it was not dirty, but it was clear this was the main bathroom used by Jack. There was a towel hanging outside the shower, inside there was a bottle of shower gel, beard shampoo and hair shampoo, some beauty products in the cupboard above the sink and all the things one would expect to find in a toilet - toilet paper, cleaning wipes, a bottle of disinfectant beside the toilet bowl.

In the bedroom, there was nothing really interesting in the bedside table - a table lamp, a phone charger, a small electronic clock. The bed was made. On the opposite side, close to the window, there was a big wardrobe and a chest of drawers. Hildegard opened them both, moved some things around and closed it. I could hear her saying something that sounded like the word 'interesting', but she did not elaborate any further.

We finally entered the living room and I was extremely excited to be there. It looked very different than the last time I was near it - for one, the body was not there anymore. There was an immense amount of clues everywhere to be seen, like a big stain on the carpet where the glass had fallen. Numbers had been placed all over the areas that were considered interesting, and I could spot number ten in one of the signs. I didn't even know where to start. I was expecting Hildegard to produce a suitcase full of examining tools and instruct me where to start scanning the room for the tiniest strand of hair, but she seemed very blase about it and it was not long until she said:

"Ok, there is nothing else for us here."

I was visibly deflated. Hildegard turned to me, with a curious look in her eyes.

"Did you actually expect us to get down on our knees with a magnifying glass and collect dust samples?"

"Maybe. I just thought we would spend more time here, after all this is the place someone died!"

"Mate, the police did that already. With people that are way more qualified than us both, and with more resources too."

"But what if they missed something?"

“And then what, do you think we would magically find a clue that a whole team of forensic analysts missed? Alright, let's say for a moment that we did. What do you think would happen then? We could just come to a judge and say we have the solution? No, no. There is a process, it needs to be documented, checked... A judge would not accept my word because I said so, no matter how good of a detective I am. A good defence attorney would never allow that to happen either. We need to think long term here.”

I was a bit disappointed. This was not how I was expecting our time at the crime scene to go.

“The actual work is already being done, we don’t need to do it again. We can stay and sift through the crime scene, or we can spend our time doing something useful, like getting something to eat, and later just look at the reports at the station. If we are still unsatisfied then, we can come back and get on our knees with the gadgets. Although I don’t think it will come to that.”

Five minutes later, we were sitting at a little cafe type of restaurant, still at the Marina, enjoying some delicious Italian food.

"Mrs Hildegard, what are we doing here? What is our role? If we read the police reports, what can we do that they can't?"

"We can think. We can understand. We can ask questions and put things together. We find the holes, the ripped pieces of fabric."

I might have looked even more lost, so Hildegard went into speech mode. She spoke like she was addressing a crowd, in a keynote type of way.

"You see, a murder is like a cloth, a piece of fabric. Everything that happens is imprinted there, and if we were to find the cloth as it is, we would have the solution right in front of our eyes. No work required. A murderer knows that, so they work to remove patches from the cloth - the patches that can incriminate them. Those patches can be removed by being ripped off or by neat cutting - the neater it is, the better for the murderer. After the patches are removed, there is a hole to be filled by the murderer. And here again, the neater the filling is done, the better for them. But no filling will make the cloth look *exactly* like it did before. It can be sawn almost perfectly together, it can be glued, but there will always be a little tip, a little end of the thread, a little spot of glue. This is what we will look for. Once you find the end tip of the thread, you can start pulling it and undo the whole thing, revealing the hole in the fabric. Once we have the hole, we work to fill it. We make theories and test them, and we use the ones that work."

"I never thought of it this way."

"But I bet you are thinking now that the end tip of the thread is an eyelash, a fingerprint... And you are not entirely wrong. But that might not always be the case. Sometimes, it's less physical and more psychological."

"I think I can see what you mean."

"I would like to share with you probably the most important thing you should know as an investigator: the three things that a murderer can manipulate. I call it the three sides of a murder."

"The three sides of a murder? I never heard about this - and I spent the last six months studying all things crime related."

"You shouldn't have heard about it, as this is a theory I developed myself. In all my years working as an investigator, both at the police and now privately, I was never proven wrong. As long as the theory stands, I will keep swearing by it. I might need to work on the name though."

"So what are the three sides of a murder?"

"These are the three aspects of a crime that someone can manipulate. First, you have the obvious one: the clues, the physical, tangible, material details. Wiping fingerprints, cleaning up blood. We live in the era of CCTV and DNA, it has become incredibly hard to manipulate evidence. Still, this is the easiest one to manipulate, but equally, it is the easiest manipulation to be discovered. I should add that this is also the most accepted in court - and this part is very important. Any good case must be able to be held in court. Our job, as investigators, is to find out who did it, and have that person arrested. But it does not end there: they will be judged and, hopefully, convicted. If we don't do our job well, they might get away later, and all our work will have been in vain."

"I confess that I haven't thought so far ahead."

"We don't tend to. In all mystery books, movies, all we want to see is the criminal being arrested. And often we are satisfied by the arrest and the statement of the main detective. But what happens next? How will that theory be proved in a trial?"

"Fascinating. Alright, evidence is the first one. What is the second one?"

"The second aspect is time, or what is called the alibi. Nobody can be at two different places at the same time, which means that someone committing a crime has to be able to manipulate time in order to appear to be somewhere else. This can be easy or hard to manipulate, depending on the situation. It can also equally be easy or difficult to prove in court. An alibi often depends on other people, as we know very well, people lie. But there are other ways to prove or disprove an alibi."

"Like CCTV."

"That's the obvious one, but also things like card payment receipts, cell phone usage... Anything that can show where someone was at some point. Now, the third and most difficult aspect to manipulate is the psychology of the crime. The previous two were the *how*, this one is the *why*. The vast majority of investigations get stuck here. What were the motives? Who wanted that person dead? Why would that person be killed? A good criminal would be able to successfully manipulate this aspect and make it hold in court. I could call it a triangle because a person who can manipulate all three aspects will be able to get away with the perfect crime."

"But there are no such things as perfect crimes."

"Are there not? Some crimes remain unsolved for years, and some will never be solved. I would argue these are perfect crimes.

Some people have come very close to achieving it, and they all had something in common: besides evidence and time, they also managed to manipulate the psychology of the crime. I remember one case when I was starting my career, where a man wanted to murder his wife, but decided to murder at least three other innocent people and pretended to be a serial killer, in order to divert attention from her death. It took a lot of great detective work to figure it out."

"How did you figure it out?"

"Oh, no. That was not me. I was just starting then. I am surprised you'd think that. Maybe one day I will introduce you to the woman who solved it, and she will tell you about it herself. Now that we are well fed and well read, are you ready to go?"

We just about finished eating, paid and made our way to the bus stop in the direction of the station. I had a big smile on my face. Yes, the fact that I had my first proper food in the last forty eight hours helped. But probably the main reason for my good mood was that I felt like, in the last half an hour, I learned more about solving a crime than I did in six months of studying. I was ready to go back and face Steve again.

Chapter Five

Everyone is innocent...

We arrived at the station around two thirty PM. At that point I had been awake for almost twelve hours, and I started to feel it taking its toll. The fact that we just had lunch did not make it easier to keep my eyes open. Felicity told me Steve was out and would be back at a quarter past three, and Hildegard decided to use this time to go to her office. Her office was located in the North Laines, about fifteen minutes walk from the police station, relatively close to the train station.

I decided to use this time to have a power nap, in order to be well rested for the rest of that Tuesday afternoon. Felicity indicated to me a side room used as a quiet area - well, as quiet as it can be inside a police station - and I found myself a cosy sofa. It did not take me long to sleep, although it was not a deep sleep. I was awoken by the sound of a man speaking with a hint of a French accent. He was loud, but sounded very polite and calm.

"Yes, Ms Porter, I will wait. I took some time free this afternoon, after I heard about the tragedy with Monsieur Jack. Such a lovely and bright boy, I cannot believe he was taken away from us so soon. Poor James, I don't know if he can take any other blow."

"Detective Pritchard will be with you in five minutes."

"Thank you, Madame."

I recognised him as Mr Cedric Dupont, the partner of Lord Honeywell. I had seen him in the media before, and I also had a feeling I saw him recently, but my head was still turning back on after my nap. Maybe I dreamed about him? I was caught in my thoughts when Steve entered the room. He looked and sounded in a better mood.

"Ah, good afternoon, Mr Dupont. Or as you frenchmen say: Bonjour."

"Bonjour Detective. I am actually Belgian, but I have been confused with French so many times that I almost feel like one. I came to offer my assistance in the case. I still cannot believe what happened to poor Jack."

"We are currently treating his death as 'under suspicious circumstances', it's too early to say if there is any foul play involved. But I would be glad to take a statement, if you would be available."

"Of course, although I don't think there is a need for that at the moment. I won't be able to add anything useful, as I haven't seen Jack since our office's Christmas party a couple of weeks ago. In any case, please do call me if you need anything. I left my card with your secretary."

I don't think Felicity liked to be referred to as secretary, and her face certainly reflected that. Mr Dupont was leaving when Steve called him back in a cool and relaxed tone, although I thought his intention was to seem blase and catch the lawyer off guard. I was starting to see what Hildegard meant by his ability to charm people.

"Pardon me, Mr Dupont, how foolish of me to forget to ask you something... But would you be able to, if we need later, of course, to state your whereabouts yesterday? Of course, if it comes to that."

"Certainly, Detective. I could do it now, if you'd like."

"Well, if it would not be an inconvenience, I guess we would get it out of the way. And if we don't need it, we at least have had all of our bases covered."

"Not a problem at all, let me just call my secretary and see if I could stay a little bit longer. I will be back in a second."

He took his phone out and made a call.

"Allo, Anna? How is my schedule looking this afternoon? The detective would like me to stay a little longer. Oh, oui? I see. Ok, thank you. I'll see you soon."

He put the phone back into his pocket and addressed Steve.

"I must apologise, detective, but I have a client waiting for me. He came in unexpectedly, so we will have to leave this statement for another time."

"Of course, I understand. Well, we have your contact, Mr Dupont. You have a nice afternoon, sir."

Steve seemed pleased with the outcome, even though it was not as he intended. Hildegard crossed Mr Dupont as he was leaving, they greeted each other, and she came in. Before she could speak, Mr Dupont came back into the room.

"Sorry, I forgot to ask you: Is Andrew still in town? I would like to have a chat with him."

"Yes, the young Mr Honeywell arrived this morning."

"This morning? That's funny. I could swear I saw him yesterday mid-afternoon in the Laines. Must have been Jack. Those boys, it's like they are twins, they always get me confused. Anyway, he's probably at his dad's, I'll pop in to see him later."

With that, he left. Hildegard grinned.

"So the lawyer came in voluntarily. Typical."

"He offered to give a statement and everything. But when it came to it, he bailed with some lame excuse. Just as I expected him to."

"Well done, detective!"

That last remark did not go down well with Steve - and I could see why, as she sounded a bit patronising. I was trying to understand why they were pleased, and Steve explained it to me.

"He is a lawyer, and an experienced one for that matter. He knows that a statement has a legal weight. He probably knows more than he is willing to share. Or else, he is being extra careful until more is found. Which, for me, is equally suspicious."

Hildegard raised the next point.

"I agree with every single thing you said. It's interesting, though, how he mentioned seeing Andrew yesterday. He likely knew Andrew was not in town, which is why I cannot help but wonder the reason for this name drop. Why didn't he want to mention that he saw Jack alive? Or did he actually want to casually mention he saw Jack alive but did not want to seem too obvious? Which, to echo the detective's words, is equally suspicious to me. We should keep an eye on that one. Anyway, where are we at?"

"Well, although we know the person living there was Jack, the victim is yet to be formally identified. Andrew is coming at four, he should probably be arriving any time soon. He will be the best person to do it, as Jack's father is in a poor condition and cannot leave the house. It is also my understanding that Andrew stayed with Jack during the holidays, so he had seen him recently. Your receptionist gave her statement earlier and we are currently analysing the CCTV footage. I thought about asking her to come identify the body as well, as she could have potentially been the last person to have seen him alive, but I didn't think it necessary, as she only saw him once and for a few minutes."

"That makes sense."

"Dr Sanjay just finished his post mortem, and he will be able to give us a full briefing at five o'clock. While we wait for Andrew, would you like to read the receptionist's statement?"

He handed us both a copy and we started reading it silently. Her statement was very straightforward: Miss Hughes had been working at the office for approximately two years and four months; yesterday was a typical day, she had her lunch and nothing really happened in the afternoon. She had just finished her mid-afternoon break when a man came into the office. It was about four thirty PM. He was wearing a sport's cap, but she could tell his hair was somewhere between light brown, ginger and blond. He was also wearing sunglasses, had a beard that matched his hair colour and his face had some freckles. He asked for Mrs Helga Hildegard, but was informed that she was not at the office. He asked if she could try to contact Mrs Hildegard and find out whether she would be returning anytime soon, as he needed to talk to her urgently. She tried to call the investigator but did not get any answer, so she sent her a text. He said he would wait to see if the investigator would answer.

She then said that he must have sat down there for twenty to thirty minutes, until she got an answer from the text, saying that the investigator had no plans of returning to the office that day, and asked what was this about. She called him to the desk, told him what the text said, and he seemed frustrated - he hit the desk with his fist. He then said that he believed that his life was in danger, and wanted to hire the investigator.

Miss Hughes then offered to try and contact Mrs Hildegard again, but he said that it was getting late and he had to go, as he had to meet someone. She asked him to write down his details on a piece of paper, but he said he would call the investigator the next day instead and left.

When asked if she could state her whereabouts of the previous day, she said that apart from her hour break between twelve and one PM, she was at the office the whole day between nine AM and six PM, and she went home straight afterwards, arriving home around six thirty PM, and she did not leave until the following day. Her husband and kids could attest to that. For her lunch break, she walked to the train station to buy a sandwich and sat down at a garden nearby. The walk to the station took her approximately seven minutes, and the walk from the garden back to the office took approximately ten. And that was it.

As soon as we finished reading, Hildegard asked another one of those questions that caught me by surprise:

"Remind me how the weather was yesterday, as I was not in Brighton for most of the day."

Steve looked annoyed at the question.

"I fail to see the relevance of this information. It was sunny and freezing cold, as we are having the coldest week of the winter so far. Why are you asking?"

"Nobody asked Miss Hughes how Jack was dressed. At least I couldn't see anything about it in her statement. But it doesn't matter, the CCTV will probably show. And I can always ask her later."

This time, I was the one who spoke.

"Do you think it's important?"

"I don't know. In fact, at the moment I don't know anything, which is why I am shooting in all directions. The more details we can gather, the best. Ah, here comes the young Mr Honeywell."

Andrew was entering the room. He looked much better than when we first saw him this morning. Hildegard talked to him.

"You just missed Mr Dupont, he was looking for you."

"Ah, ok, thank you. I will call uncle Cedric later. How are you all?"

"It's been a long day, mate. But I can see you had a shower, some food, maybe a sleep?"

"I did, indeed. I love to stay at dad's, I am treated like a king. I could never understand why Jack wanted his own flat, if he could have all that."

"How is your uncle?"

"It doesn't look good, but he is receiving the best treatment money can buy. He is holding on for now, but I don't know how much longer he can endure."

His demeanour suddenly changed, when he talked about this. There was a lot of sadness in that statement. He went on.

"Since we are in the mood already, could we please do the formal identification? I want to get this part done and behind me. I don't want to remember Jack like this."

We proceeded to the morgue. Dr Sanjay was waiting for us there. He pulled the drawer where Jack's body was laying, covered by a white sheet. He pulled the part covering the body's face. Andrew looked dreadful - it was clear he hated being there; there was some resignation to his face, as this was something that had to be done. His eyes watered and he spoke, with his voice almost breaking, while a small tear rolled down his eyes.

"Oh Jack, why did it have to come to this? Yes, that is my brother Jack. I'm sorry, cousin Jack. It is odd for me to call him cousin."

"I hereby formally identify the victim as Jack Louis Honeywell."

Andrew looked away and said, with resignation.

"Now, can we please go?"

Dr Sanjay closed the drawer and we left the morgue. Steve told Andrew to take some time away, and we would regroup at five o'clock for a briefing.

Hildegard and I went to grab a coffee, probably my hundredth that day, in the cafe around the station. Hildegard spoke, and her voice was almost breaking.

"I have been doing this for almost a hundred years and I can never get used to this part. I hate the identification. It needs to be done, but I hate it."

"I think this is a good thing that you feel this way. Means you remain human inside. It's easy to dissociate and forget these are lives."

"Mate, you hit the nail in the head. You can see things in a pure, simple way. Don't ever let the years take it away from you."

At five minutes before five, Dr Sanjay joined us for his briefing. He spoke, and his voice was firm and to the point - it sounded like he was narrating a documentary.

"Good afternoon, folks. We are gonna start from the beginning. Jack Louis Honeywell, British, caucasian, thirty two years old, was found unresponsive in his residence at Brighton Marina by his next door neighbour at fifteen minutes past three AM today, the third of January. He was pronounced dead at the scene at forty five minutes past three AM of the same day."

We all heard this information before, but I guess it was his duty to include it. He continued.

"We believe the deceased was poisoned, early signs show what appear to be methanol ingestion. Toxicology analysis of the body is being conducted, and the lab will be able to give us a definitive answer tomorrow evening, maybe the day after tomorrow. I reminded them this is the utmost priority right now. We also collected samples from the carpet and the glass, in the hopes most of it had not evaporated. It was a cold day/night, we have that in our favour. I don't know what were the victim's drinking habits, meaning that this could have easily been confused with the taste of a common alcoholic beverage, especially for someone who does not drink regularly."

Andrew nodded with his head.

"He did not drink much."

"Now, based on the images from the CCTV, and the distance between the office and the Marina, I can estimate the time of death between five thirty and six PM, maybe six-fifteen."

Steve then spoke, followed by Hildegard.

"That's awfully narrow, isn't it doctor?"

"Agreed. Considering that he left my office at five PM and the time it would have taken him to get home, he would have had to be murdered right when he arrived home. Not much time to play with. I mean, it's possible, but indeed very curious."

The doctor did not seem to change his mind.

"I am sure that he could not have died after six. In fact, when I first observed the body, I judged that he had been dead for at least twelve hours, but that was purely based on a preliminary observation. These things need to be verified, tested, combined with other evidence - the footage from Mrs Hildegard's office, for example. Based on all those factors, I have established the time of death to be as wide as I could. I could throw another fifteen minutes in for the sake of the margin of error, but I would not go later than six thirty pm. There are many technical details about the scene of the crime, but I think it's worth mentioning that the lock did not seem to be damaged, which leads us to assume that the person was known by the victim."

I knew what that meant, and I was eager to show my knowledge.

"He opened the door to the killer."

"Not necessarily. It's a possibility, yes, but the killer could have been inside already. They could have had a copy of the keys, for example. Anyone you know that would have a copy, Mr Honeywell?"

"Hmm, no, not that I can think of. I mean, there is an emergency key at dad's, but Dolores is responsible for it. She should be able to tell you if anyone picked it up. I find it unlikely, as that key should have only been used for emergencies."

"It is also interesting to note that the body did not show any signs of a struggle or a fight, so it is likely that the victim and the killer had a conversation. My theory is that the killer either knocked on the door and came in, or was already waiting inside, they started talking, the killer offered the victim a drink and spiked said drink with methanol, in enough quantity to poison the victim. The killer then exited but left the door ajar."

Hildegard raised the next point.

"It is also curious that the killer would leave the door open, for the body to be discovered by a neighbour. A killer usually wants to hide their crime for as long as possible, to gain time."

"My thoughts exactly. But that seems to be the case here. No fingerprints of interest were found in the house. I say that because we did find many partial prints in different areas and on the glass where the poison was administered, but those might have been there already from previous usages."

Something came into my mind, and I asked the next question.

"Wouldn't washing the glass remove the prints?"

"Depends on how the glass is washed. We all know Jack used a dishwasher, and there is a discussion amongst the forensic community on whether a dishwasher can completely remove prints and DNA. There is a possibility for them to resist cleaning. That would be consistent with the faint partials we found in the glass."

Hildegard raised an interesting point.

"Here we might want to go back to the weather yesterday. It was a cold day, so it is possible our assailant would be wearing gloves. It would have been unusual to wear them inside, but not impossible."

"Apart from that, we all know the rest. The body was discovered by Miss Alisson Ling when she was returning home from a night out."

"I bet she's happy now."

Andrew spoke, and by the look on his face, his mouth acted faster than his brain again. Hildegard looked at him with a curious glance.

"What do you mean, Andrew?"

"Oh, erm, no, it's probably nothing."

"Anything is of vital importance on this stage. Please, speak up."

"Jack and the neighbour had some issues. I heard them arguing when I was staying over."

Steve intervened.

"Mr Honeywell, I would like to take your statement next, and I would certainly like you to tell us more about this. But first, Dr Sanjay, do you have anything else to add?"

"No, that is pretty much everything we know at this point. I will keep you updated as soon as I hear anything else. Now, if you don't need me anymore, I gotta go. Pryia and I have an OBGYN appointment at six."

"By all means, my dear doctor. Give your wife our best."

Dr Sanjay thanked us all and left. Steve turned to Andrew.

"Are you ready to give us a statement?"

"Are you gonna flash a light on my face?"

I thought to myself: 'Oh Andrew! Count to five in your head before you say something!' He gave a yellow smile, probably realising he had done it again, and continued in a more serious tone.

"Yes, I am ready."

"My name is Stephen Pritchard, I am the Lead Investigator in the investigation into the death of Jack Honeywell. This is a voluntary interview and it is being recorded in writing by Felicity Browne-Porter, Assistant Investigator. You are not considered a suspect at this point, but we are treating everyone involved in this case as a person of interest. Therefore, I am putting you under caution. This means you can end this interview anytime and you do not have to say anything. However, it may harm your defence if you do not mention when questioned something which you later rely on in court. Anything you do say may be given in evidence. You will have a chance to read and sign a copy of the transcript of your interview once it is over. Finally, I would like to remind you that you have the right to legal representation before proceeding. Do you understand and agree to start?"

"Yes, I do."

“Let’s start from the beginning then. When did you last see Jack?”

“Ok, the beginning. I was staying with him until the twenty ninth of december. I came over for the office’s Christmas party on the twentieth, but I went back home that day. It’s just an hour and a half with the train, which made it easy for me to go back and sleep at home, as I had to work the following day. I then arrived in Brighton on Christmas eve, and we both stayed at dad’s for Christmas and Boxing Day. We left on the twenty-seventh, but I decided to spend some time at my brother’s. He was doing some part-time work for a charity, working from home, and I stayed around doing nothing, enjoying my time off. “

“Is there any particular reason you decided to stay with your cousin?”

“We don’t get to see each other very often anymore, now that I live away. It was good for bonding. I also wanted to talk to Jack about some stuff, like dad’s health.”

"And you mentioned an argument between Jack and Miss Ling?"

"Yes. I don't really know what happened, I only heard parts of the conversation. I believe Jack left her a note under her door, and she came over to talk about it. I was at the shower, and when I finished I could hear their voices altered. Jack was saying that he had had enough and he would inform the Marina Management and her landlord about it, and there was nothing for them to discuss anymore. He said something about giving her many chances, how she wasted them, and she should be grateful he was not taking this any further. She then threatened him, saying that he did not know the kind of people she was connected with, and that he should not mess with her. I left the bathroom right when he was closing the front door, but I heard her screaming from outside, something like how she didn't judge his choices, he shouldn't judge hers either."

"Were those her exact words?"

"Maybe, or something in that direction. I asked him what happened, and if he was ok, but he said it was just neighbour stuff, I should not worry about it."

"And when was that?"

"On the twenty-eight of December."

"Did anyone else come to the house while you were there?"

"No, not that I can remember now."

"And that was the twenty-ninth the last time you saw him?"

"I mean, I did see him today in the morgue."

He answered it with a kind of awkward smile, as if he was trying to use humour to deflect being under pressure. Steve did not seem amused.

"This is no time for humour, Mr Honeywell."

"My apologies, detective. It's not easy to be put in the spot like this, especially on a day like today. It doesn't help that you keep me calling Mr Honeywell either. Please call me Andrew"

"Let's proceed: after you left Brighton, what happened?"

"I went back home, as I would have to work for the next three days. I had a half day off on the thirty-first and a late start on the first of January, but I did not have the time off, as I used it for Christmas. Much of my colleagues were away, I was covering for them. I spent New Year's Eve at a friend's house but left shortly after the firework display on the TV at midnight. I walked to and from my friend's place. I also walk to work. You see, I live in a small town, so it's easier to walk everywhere. Sometimes I like to bike, but the weather is not great for biking at the moment."

"Right. What about yesterday, Andrew? Can you recount your whereabouts yesterday, January second, with as many details as you can?"

"I worked from nine AM to twelve PM, but I did not feel very well. My manager then sent me home. I believe that, with all this travelling and all this walking around in this weather, I was coming down with a cold. I had a headache and my body was aching as well. Could have been a hangover, as I went for a couple of drinks the night before, but I would not tell my manager that. I arrived home around twelve twenty-five PM, knocked at Mrs Kensignton's door and asked her for some headache medicine and some tea. She said I looked poorly, and gave me some pills, some tea, honey and a handful of cakes. She told me to take a good bath and try to sleep this off, so I did. I must have slept the whole afternoon, because I woke up at seven PM with Mrs Kensington knocking at my door. I opened the door and asked her what she gave me, as it had knocked me out. She said it was one of her migraine pills, and it made sense, as she knocked earlier and I didn't answer. To be fair, I think I heard her knocking around four o'clock, but the thought of leaving my blankets and engaging in conversation with her did not appeal to me. I stayed in that night, in order to recover myself properly. I woke up today at seven AM with a call from Dolores informing me that someone was found dead at Jack's flat, but they did not have much information yet."

"And you called Mrs Hildegard, asking if your cousin had contacted her yet, and if she would be willing to join the case, as you thought foul play was involved. What made you think so?"

"Correct. It was a conversation I had with Jack on the first of January over the phone. He told me he was feeling threatened and he was scared for his life. He told me 'if I end up dead, don't trust anyone and look over your shoulder'. I thought it was paranoia, but I told him to go to the police. He said he did not want to involve the police on it, he would prefer this to be handed privately, as it involved something sensitive that could be damaging if it got out. I then remembered an article I read in The Guardian about how Mrs Hildegard was being honoured with a medal in London this week, with a profile of her and her cases, and that she lived in Brighton, so I suggested he contact her."

"Did Jack elaborate further on why he thought his life was in danger?"

"No, he said he did not want to involve me, to protect me. He just told me to be careful and trust no one around me."

"Interesting. I assume you are staying at your uncle's?"

"Yes, Jack and I will always have a bed at dad's. I might need to pop back into Essex for a thing or two, but as I said, the train ride is less than two hours long. I should be around."

"I have one last question for you, Andrew."

"Yes?"

"Can you think of someone who would like to see your brother dead?"

"I think it's easier to think of who wouldn't. Jack was not a bad person, he did not have any enemies, but with dad dying, he became the centre of it all. Many things will be transferred to him. It's a lot of responsibility and a lot to be dealt with, and the people around dad are not the best group in the world, if you know what I mean."

"That does not help us much."

"There is something else, but I don't know if I should say anything about it. It's not really any of my business."

"Anything you can share is crucial, Andrew. Remember, your cousin is dead and we have no leads."

"Yes, you're right. Jack was having an affair with a married woman. But not any married woman, he was having an affair with Mrs Smith, dad's secretary. Her husband found out, and he was not happy about it."

"Didn't Jack have a girlfriend?"

"Lily? No, she broke up with him after the Christmas party."

"That is very interesting. Gives us a place to start."

"Yeah, the neighbour and the husband, I would start there. I am not saying either of them killed him, but I don't think either of them are mourning his death, if you know what I mean."

"This is the end of the interview. Thank you very much, Andrew. This has been very helpful, indeed. Felicity will print you a copy for you to sign."

She printed the statement, handed it to Andrew with a pen and he started to sign it, but the pen didn't seem to work. He tried it once again a bit more forcefully, until the pen broke in his hand, spilling ink in the paper and staining the sleeve of his shirt.

Felicity apologised profusely, but he looked amused with the situation.

"Don't worry, it happens. I am going home anyway, it's not like I have a date. Although I could show this stain and say I got this at a police station, that would be a sign of virility, right?"

He flexed his right arm as he said it, making the stained sleeve come close to his bicep. We all laughed at that moment of levity, in a way we were all learning to appreciate the way he used humour as a mechanism of deflection when things got too serious. Felicity printed another copy, handed him with a pen she tested beforehand, and he signed it, making sure the stain would not touch the paper.

"Can I do anything else for you, detective? Otherwise I will go home, we are about to release a statement to the press, and I would like to oversee that. Dad is in no condition to do anything these days."

"No, Andrew, you are free to go. Thank you very much for your cooperation. Keep your phone on, will you?"

"Absolutely."

After Andrew left, I turned to Steve.

"I have a classroom question: Why did you put him under caution? I thought we only did that to suspects, not witnesses."

"You are right, kid. But at the moment we don't know much about the case, so I am treating everyone as a person of interest, as a potential suspect. It's an extra precaution, in case we need it at some point. If we don't, no harm will be done. He had the chance to remain silent or to decline doing the interview altogether. I think we should cover all our bases - especially now."

He was referring to the fact that the news was about to get out to the press, and we started bracing ourselves for what was about to come our way.

...until proven otherwise

Nevertheless, Steve looked very excited, which I could not understand how, especially after being awake for so long.

"Wow, that was a statement! We now have somewhere to start."

Hildegard followed his mood and enthusiasm.

"Indeed it was. Mate, there is a lot to unpack here. How unlucky that Jack went to see me yesterday, the day I was in London getting the medal - the one Andrew mentioned. I would have loved to hear what he had to say."

"We will have a little window into that - I saved the best for last! It's time to watch the footage of him at your office."

We went to another room, where there was a TV and some video equipment. Dr Sanjay had left everything ready for us. It was only Steve, Hildegard and me in the room. Felicity was not interested in watching the footage, so Steve asked her to do a little something for him, telling him she could go home afterwards.

He started the video, and the footage showed a small timestamp on the upper right corner of the image. It was showing sixteen colon twenty-eight colon forty-nine, and right under it the letters MON and the numbers zero two slash zero one. It showed a typical reception area, with a door on the right side of the image and the reception desk on the left. On the upper side of the image, there was a sofa by a wall, with a generic painting above it. The street outside looked busy, but it was not possible to identify anyone passing due to the quality of the image.

Miss Hughes sat at her desk, doing what one would expect from a receptionist. The door suddenly opened and a man entered, coming from the left side of the building. It was clear to anyone who's seen Jack that it was him, but it was not possible to discern his hair or beard colour, as the footage was in black and white. I could see how this would be what his hair and beard would look like on black and white image, though. He was wearing jeans trousers, a thick winter jacket, sunglasses and a sports cap.

He approached the receptionist table and started to talk to her. There was no sound. He was gesticulating as he was in distress, a little bit over dramatic in my opinion - but then again, I was not afraid for my life, who was I to judge? Miss Hughes made a call, then picked up her phone and texted. She said something to Jack, and he took a seat on the couch.

Steve then fast forwarded the footage, because nothing much happened. One person came in to drop a package but left shortly, Miss Hughes picked up calls, and she would occasionally talk to him, but it did not look like they had a full conversation.

Around four fifty-seven, Steve restarted the footage on the normal speed. Miss Hughes seemed to call Jack up to the desk, told him something, he took off his sunglasses, shook his head and pounded his right fist down vigorously. Miss Hughes produced a piece of paper and a pen, tried to hand him but he refused, shook his head, spoke some other words and left, returning his sunglasses to his face. He exited the door and turned right.

Steve then spoke with a hint of sarcasm.

"There you have it, Mrs Hildegard. The mystery of what Jack was wearing."

"You mock me, my good detective, but there is something there. I have a gut feeling. It doesn't matter."

"Well, I think we can finish for today. It has been a long day, and I for one need a pint and a 'fag'. Anyone would like to accompany me to the pub across the street?"

Hildegard smiled and spoke politely.

"Much appreciated for the invitation, but I will have to decline. Jill is preparing her world famous spag bol and I do not want to miss that. My wife makes the absolute best spag bol. She says she cooks everything for hours, but I am convinced she uses those powder seasoning bags. I never caught her though. In any case, I will have a glass of wine tonight, and we will toast to you, your pint and your cigarette."

"I, for one, will go into my furnished flat and enjoy some takeaway on my own."

I said that with the hopes of being invited to Hildegard's dinner, but the invitation didn't come. And the idea of accompanying Steve to a pub was dreadful to me, so I resigned myself to being alone at home. Steve didn't seem to care.

"Very well. I shall see you two tomorrow at ten-thirty AM. I have to be here earlier to do some admin work, and you're welcome to join, but the good stuff won't start until eleven, when Miss Ling is coming back to clarify her argument with the victim. I am curious to what she will say, but mostly to why she said she never talked to him in the first place."

We said our goodbyes and left. I got home and ordered myself a pizza, got a glass of wine and prepared a bath. My bath coincided with the time it took for the pizza to be delivered, and I sat myself in front of the TV to eat and watch some news. It wasn't a surprise that the death of Jack dominated the news that evening. Nobody talked about anything else for the first fifteen minutes of the segment. There were not many details about the crime, but that didn't stop the speculation. Reporters appeared live from the Marina and the police station - they must have arrived after we left. Then there was a recap on the life of Lord Honeywell and finally, the statement from the family was read. The family lamented to inform that Mr Jack Honeywell was found dead and the circumstances of the death were being investigated by the police. The family asked for privacy in this difficult moment. I was fascinated by the irony - the media making a spectacle of it all while saying that the family asked for privacy.

Falling asleep came very easily that night, as it had been an early morning for me. I slept deep and don't remember dreaming. The first time I opened my eyes was around eight-twenty AM, as my bladder insisted on reminding me of the two glasses of wine I had before going to bed. I made myself a cup of coffee and a bowl of porridge, and went back to the couch in front of the TV. The news, once again, was dominated by the death. Alleged suspects, statements from the police, interview with specialists. Live reporting from the Marina showed the people had been lighting candles and depositing flowers in front of the building. Others reported live from across the family home in Hove, where some flowers have also been deposited. There seemed to be a vast number of reporters in front of the station, and they went live to show the arrival of Steve. He did not give any interview, and said an official bulletin would be released in the afternoon. I was dreading going there when I got a call from Hildegard.

"Mate, I assume you've seen the circus in front of the station?"

"I did. How are we ever getting in?"

"There is a service door that not a lot of people know about. I guess our good detective did not watch the news, that dumb man. How could he have not thought it would be packed?"

"Maybe he wanted the attention?"

"Maybe. I certainly don't. Do you?"

"Absolutely not!"

"That's what I thought. Meet me at the Pavilion at ten and we go in together."

We met punctually at ten in front of the Brighton Pavilion and walked to the police station together, but through a different route that I did not know. There was a small door in the backside of the building, in front of a closed parking area for police cars, and we used it to enter the building. We walked up the stairs and arrived at our usual room. Steve seemed to be in a horrible mood, as always. He was talking on the phone, Hildegard started to chat with Felicity and I came to the window to have a look at the street in front of the station. It was packed with reporters, cars parked everywhere showing the logos of TV and radio stations. The street had been closed to cars, with police officers on both ends controlling the flux with traffic cones.

The commotion seemed to draw attention from the people working in the American Express building in front of us. I saw people on the phone, sitting by the window, looking at their computers, but also trying to keep up with what was happening outside. A man with brown beard, designer glasses and a black pullover worked at a desk by the window a couple of floors above my line of view, and when he saw me, he waved his hand. I felt like a celebrity staying at a hotel. But my fame moment did not last long, as Steve called us.

"Good morning, everyone. Welcome to day two of hell. As you can see, now we have the press at our door. Everything now will be scrutinised and dissected by the worst kind of people in this country: tabloid reporters; needless to say, everything mentioned in this room stays here. We only tell the world what we agree on. Do we have an understanding?"

The three of us, Felicity, Hildegard and myself nodded. Steve went on.

"Dr Sanjay is the only other person who knows what goes inside this room. And of course the commissioner, who we have to report to. Now, for today's agenda. As you are all aware, Miss Ling is coming at eleven AM. I also Invited Miss Lilian Ahmet to come over and give us a statement, she should be in at twelve PM. Miss Ahmet was Jack's girlfriend, so we are treating them both as persons of interest at this point. Dr Sanjay is chasing the toxicology reports and might be able to give us an update later this afternoon."

At ten minutes past eleven, Steve started to look at his watch impatiently. He was about to make a call when Allison Ling entered the room.

"Sorry, matey. Impossible to come in, the street is taken. It's mad!"

"Welcome, Miss Ling. I mean, Ali."

"Thank you. Hullo y'all."

"My name is Stephen Pritchard, I am the Lead Investigator in the investigation into the death of Jack Honeywell. This is a voluntary interview and it is being recorded in writing by Felicity Browne-Porter, Assistant Investigator. You are not considered a suspect at this point, but we are treating everyone involved in this case as a person of interest. Therefore, I am putting you under caution. This means you can end this interview anytime and you do not have to say anything. However, it may harm your defence if you do not mention when questioned something which you later rely on in court. Anything you do say may be given in evidence. You will have a chance to read and sign a copy of the transcript of your interview once it is over. Finally, I would like to remind you that you have the right to legal representation before proceeding. Do you understand and agree to start?"

"Oi, I said ev'rything already. I din't know that bloke."

"Ali, I need your confirmation that you understand what I just said to you, and that you are willing to proceed."

"Yeah, ok. I confirm."

"Excellent. When you were last here, you said that you did not know Jack very well, and that you had never spoken to him other than the occasional greeting in the corridor. I have been informed that you and Jack had an argument, I believe on the twenty-eight of December. Is that correct?"

"Argument? Nah, don't remember."

"Well, let me remind you then. I got the information that Jack said he would inform the marina management and your landlord about something, and you said something about how he should not mess with you. Could you clarify that?"

Alisson looked astonished. She was entirely caught by surprise. She stuttered.

"Erm.. well... That... No, I got nothing to say about that."

"No problem. Is there *anything* you would like to say to us that you haven't before? Or do you want to end this interview?"

"I don't know why you're on to me like that, I was not the one screaming at 'im, saying stuff like 'if I can't be with you, nobody will' for ev'ryone in the building to hear. That's the fight ya shoul'be worrying yo'selves with."

"Who said that?"

"That girlfriend of 'is. Ha, she din't know the stuff 'e did when she was not around. Bloody idiot she was. But it's none of ma'business, 'e can do what 'e wants with 'is life. Sometimes peoples gotta do what they gotta do."

"And when was that?"

"Same day, matey. Bit earlier than our 'argument', d'ya know what I'm sayin'?"

"So you *did* have an argument with Mr Jack."

"Ya know, matey, I don't wanna say an'thing anymore. You you'self said I didn't have to answer, I won't answer any of that stuff. I want to end this chat now."

"No problem, Miss Ling. I am concluding this interview and you are not under caution anymore. I will have your statement printed for you to sign before you go."

"I ain't signing any bloody thing."

"Do as you wish. But bear in mind that you gave this statement in front of two members of the police, one person working for the police and a private investigator who's name is known by everyone in this country. We could still show everyone in a trial that you refused to sign it, and testify to what we heard. It would be the word of four people against one, four people that work with law enforcement. If you want to bet on those chances, it's your choice. Of course, there is always a chance that *your* word will be the one they believe."

Ali looked defeated. I felt uncomfortable with that intimidation, even though every word of it made sense. On the other hand, we had a potential murderer there, refusing to talk, when she was informed that this statement was voluntary and that it would be valid in the eyes of the justice. It was not easy to take her side.

She signed the form, got up and started walking towards the exit. Hildegard called her, her voice was friendly, but firm.

"I would like to ask you a question, Miss Ling. I believe one of your friends told one of our informants that you did not really stay the whole time in Portslade that afternoon, as you said before. In fact, I believe you left them at around four pm and only reunited with them around seven. Am I right to believe that? And if I am, why would you not have informed us about it in your previous statement?"

The colour suddenly disappeared from Ali's face. She looked like she had seen a ghost, her mouth opened but no word came out of it. She finally spoke.

"Blimey, how on the 'ell did you lot discover these things? I bet it was Katie, that girl is a snitch. I'll show her what is good, I will."

Steve raised his voice.

"Miss Ling, may I remind you that you are inside a police station, in front of police officers."

He muttered something like 'whatever', got up and started towards the exit. Hildegard addressed her one last time.

"Miss Ling, off the record, could I give you a piece of advice?"

"What's that?"

"Get yourself a lawyer. A good one."

Her face relaxed a bit, and she left. I turned to Hildegard and asked how *did* she know about the time away from the friends. Steve was the one who answered.

"I think it was a hunch, am I right?"

"You are absolutely right."

"It is all a matter of phrasing it. Hildegard never affirmed anything, she said that she believed. She can believe whatever she wants. She can believe that the sky is purple. It doesn't mean it is. These are two very different things."

I could not believe what I heard. I felt this was unfair play, or even worse.

"Is that legal?"

"In this case, yes. All I did was express an opinion. A belief. Opinions and beliefs are not facts. Besides, Ali knew from the beginning that she could have stayed quiet and said nothing. She was also not under caution anymore, so that is all off the record. We cannot use any of that in court. But I felt it was important to know, so we can build a better picture of her alibi. And I think the detective agrees with me on this one?"

"I do. Sometimes you have to sacrifice a pawn to win the game later."

I was still not convinced.

"How about when you practically forced her to sign the statement, is that ok?"

"When we asked her to sign the statement, I made sure to say something very important, something that will make all the difference. I again gave her the choice not to sign it."

I could not remember that part, but he refreshed my memory.

"Oh, but I did. I used the phrase 'Of course, there is always a chance that your word will be the one they believe' exactly."

"But everyone could hear your sarcastic tone."

"Sarcasm is subjective. But, most importantly, it's not noted on the statement. We only write the words, not how they were spoken."

"This is all very sneaky and cunning."

Hildegard was the one who addressed my concerns. She sounded very impatient.

"So is murdering someone. We are trying to catch that murderer. Which side are you on? We did not torture anyone, we simply used clever questioning techniques. Don't make this bigger than it is."

Chapter Seven
Nothing to see here

I felt silly for having raised it. She was right. In the grand scheme of things, we wanted to catch a murderer. Felicity brought us a round of coffees and teas, and that relaxed the atmosphere a little bit. We had to get ready for our next person of interest, Lilian Ahmet.

Lily, as she was called by everyone, was only daughter of Mr Rachid Ahmet, a Lebanese millionaire who owned the biggest chain of pubs in England. She came into Jack's life through his father, who defended Mr Ahmet in a case of embezzlement against the government. Mr Ahmet would usually tell everyone that half his fortune was honorarily owned by Lord Honeywell, as long as the latter would not touch it. After the case, the Ahmets invited the Honeywells for a summer holiday trip in their estate in the Lebanese countryside, in a village by the outskirts of Bhamdum. Lily attracted the attention of both the boys, but ended up dating Jack. They had broken up recently. Lily called herself a social media influencer, and all that information about her, her father, and his relationship with Jack and his family was public, in her blog, for anyone to read.

When she entered the room, we were all mesmerised by her beauty. She looked like a middle eastern princess, out of a story book. Dark, thick and long black hair in a ponytail, that shone a slight hue of blue under the light; equally dark and thick eyebrows covering dark brown eyes and noticeable makeup, especially around the eyes, with black lines that extended their shape. Her nose was prominent, the mouth had full lips that looked artificial.

She was dressed in less of a princess and more of a modern 'it' girl look, wearing a sweatpants/sweatshirt combination that showed a big logo brand; her sunglasses and purse also showed prominent brands. I had the impression I was looking at a woman version of a cat dressed in brand names, going on holiday.

She sat down in front of Steve, removed her sunglasses, set her hair free and shook her head in a subtle way that reminded me of a hair conditioner advertisement. It was all very fake and staged, like she was being filmed for a reality TV show. Steve waited for all the theatrics to end and then addressed her.

“Good afternoon, Miss Ahmet. Thank you for coming today.”

“Hmm, why am I here again?”

“My name is Stephen Pritchard, I am the Lead Investigator in the investigation into the death of Jack Honeywell. This is a voluntary interview and it is being recorded in writing by Felicity Browne-Porter, Assistant Investigator. You are not considered a suspect at this point, but we are treating everyone involved in this case as a person of interest. Therefore, I am putting you under caution. This means you can end this interview anytime and you do not have to say anything. However, it may harm your defence if you do not mention when questioned something which you later rely on in court. Anything you do say may be given in evidence. You will have a chance to read and sign a copy of the transcript of your interview once it is over. Finally, I would like to remind you that you have the right to legal representation before proceeding. Do you understand and agree to start?"

"A person of interest?"

"I need verbal confirmation that you understand what I said and you agree to proceed."

"I sure do and I don't mind, detective. I have nothing to hide, my life is an open book. You can't have close to two hundred thousand followers and expect privacy. It's the price to pay."

She said that last phrase with the air of a martyr. Felicity, who was taking notes, rolled her eyes. The detective ignored it and started talking.

"Now, to answer your question, you were in a relationship with the victim, and as one of the closest people to him, it is natural we would like to ask you questions."

"Babe, you can't be serious. You think *I* killed Jack? Ha! Can you imagine?"

"We don't think anything, Miss Ahmet. At the moment we are making investigations, asking questions, trying to get the facts and understand the circumstances. At least at this stage."

"Well, I didn't kill Jack. Even if I wanted to, I would have gotten someone to do it. Get my hands dirty with blood, ew. No, I didn't do it. Is that all?"

"Not quite. I understand you and the deceased were in a relationship, but it ended recently?"

"You understand correctly, we were. But I broke it off last month."

"Would you care to elaborate?"

"Jack was sleeping with a married woman - you should be grilling her, not me, by the way. His dad's secretary. How disgusting, how common, how typical straight white male. Fucking his dad's secretary, ugh. Do you know what that could do to my brand? Jack was useful, but not enough for me to have to deal with this."

"Please mind your language, Miss Ahmet. Now, are you referring to Mrs Anna Smith?"

"Is that her name?"

Hildegard opened her purse, took out a picture and put it on the table. It was the picture I had seen on the board, above the computer, in Jack's office. The one that showed Andrew on one side and Jack on the other. I have no clue how she managed to take the picture away from the board without me seeing her do so. I did recognise Lily in the picture, as the woman trying to hug Jack. I also noticed that the man standing next to Andrew was Mr Cedric Dupont, who I saw at the station after we examined the crime scene.

Steve looked very surprised by the sudden appearance of the photo, but Lily did not seem to notice, or care. He asked Lily to point to the woman she was talking about, if she was in the picture. Lily pointed to the woman hugging the man, in the middle of the picture, the third person from the left. Lily had the same look of disgust now that she had on the picture, and I could understand why.

"That's her. She's not even that cute. I wonder how many followers she has."

"How did you find out about this alleged affair?"

"Andrew saw them together. They were not discreet."

"And Andrew told you about it? I didn't know you two were in *these* terms."

"I don't know what you are insinuating, but Andrew and I are *just* friends. I should have gone for him, he is the good one, he would be a great husband. But he's boring. And besides, he's only the nephew. There's no pizazz."

"Why did he tell you, then?"

"To try and put some sense into Jack's head? He talked to Jack about it, but Jack denied it. Lied to his own brother, the nerve! So Andrew came to me, told me Jack didn't deserve me, that I should threaten to leave him. Men can't deal with rejection."

"And then what happened?"

"Then I told Jack that I wouldn't admit that. He denied it, but he said he was ok with the end of our relationship. I was livid! How dare he! Who did he think he was to decide when we would break up?"

"When was that?"

"Let's see, the Christmas party was on the twentieth, then I went to my parents for Christmas and then I flew to LA on the twenty-ninth, so I think it was the twenty-eight. I remember how glad I was to leave all this behind me and start the new year and the new me away from these people."

"A neighbour heard you saying the phrase 'if I can't be with you, nobody will'. Did you say that to Jack?"

"Why, yes I did, but it's not what you're thinking. I didn't mean I would kill him. Have you seen Jack? He's no prize, hun. There are not a lot of girls who want to be associated with that family, to bring James's son to their parents. I told Jack that he was *lucky* I gave him a chance, and if he couldn't make it work with me, he would die alone. I guess I was right, after all."

That last statement gave me chills. She was very blase about Jack's death. How could she be so cold about the person who she dated up to a month ago, who was now dead? Steve continued.

"Was there anyone else with him when you had this argument?"

"I think Andrew was staying with him, but I don't know if wasn't home. No, he wasn't. I'm almost sure."

"You said you flew to LA on the twenty-ninth, today is the fourth and you're already back. That's a short trip for such a long distance. Why did you come back so soon?"

"Work, babe. The job of a popular girl never stops."

"When did you get back into this country?"

"The second, in the morning."

"The day of the murder."

"Ha ha, very clever! Now before you start making accusations, I spent the day in London. This business, it doesn't stop. I had an insta session for my friend's new cupcake shop. It's all vegan and sustainable. If you don't believe me, ask the ten thousand people who watched my live that afternoon, they can vouch for me. My insta lives usually gather more than ten thousand viewers. On a bad day."

"With all due respect, Miss Ahmet, we are not interested in your fans. We are questioning *you* now. Did you sleep in London that night?"

"How rude! And no, I came home to Brighton in the evening. I had a dinner party to attend."

"What time did you arrive in Brighton?"

"Must have been four-something PM when we stopped at the station. I took an Uber home, too many bags to carry, and my assistant didn't come down with me. I gave the poor boy some days to see his family. Work life balance is very important, I don't want him to burn out on me. Too busy to deal with that."

"What time was the dinner party?"

"We met at the Ivy at seven-thirty. I didn't stay too late though, I was destroyed, after flying overnight and working the whole day.

No first class compares to one's own bed, especially not the one I took. And everyone knows how a good night's sleep is indispensable for one's beauty."

"Can you state your whereabouts between four and seven PM that day?"

"I was home. I had a long bath, uploaded some photos, answered some fanmail and had a power nap."

"Can anyone attest that you were home at this time?"

"I live alone, detective. I know, it's crazy for a pretty girl like me to live alone in a place like Brighton, but I consider myself a trailblazer. I am an inspiration for many young girls who want to make it in this world. It's not enough to be pretty anymore."

Steve seemed to be losing his patience with her, and it looked like the feeling was mutual. She snapped her fingers, impatiently.

"Can we have a wrap in this sesh? I've got tons to do this afternoon. Do you have it all or do I need to answer any more?"

"I think we have it all. This is the end of this interview and you are not under caution anymore. We might need to contact you, can you provide us the address you intend to stay for the next two weeks?"

"I will have Brenner forward you our hotel's address in Dubai."

"I would rather you'd stay in this country for the time being, Miss Ahmet."

"No can do, babe. I have to promote a new boutique hotel in Dubai. If I bail now, my reputation will be tarnished. Do you know how people can be cancelled in a matter of seconds now? Not even my Arabic would save me. There are not many British influencers who can speak perfect Arabic like me. Those tedious holidays in Lebanon paid off, I knew I had to endure them for a reason."

"I must insist, it's important you stay here while the investigations continue."

"Unless you arrest me or take away my passport, there's nothing I can do for you detective."

"I can arrange that."

"Well, you have until eight-twenty this evening. That's when my flight departs. Besides, my passport is not even here with me, my assistant Brenner takes care of that side of things. I don't know what I would do without that boy. Very clever and very efficient, like a good gay should be. Thankfully I don't need to be his beard. He'll be meeting me in Heathrow. So I guess we'll see you at the gate? Better be quick, I'm usually the first one to board."

She got up, but Steve stopped her.

"First, you need to read and sign your statement, Miss Ahmet."

Felicity printed the statement and handed it to her, she signed without even looking at it, added two times the letters "xo" to her signature and handed it back. She put her sunglasses on top of her head, got up and started to leave. But she stopped at the door and turned around. I was expecting her to add something or make another snarky remark, but she managed to surprise me once again.

“Can I take a selfie with you all? My followers are dying to know what it's like to be in a real investigation, in a real police station. So exciting!”

“We would rather keep this investigation outside social media, Miss Ahmet.”

“I don't know why, it's all over the news. But oh well, it's your loss. Lots of followers up for grabs. You, of all people, would be *very* popular online.”

She was talking to me. I felt my cheeks blushing. She said "Ciao, Belli" and left. We waited about three minutes, and without planning, all started laughing together. What a bizarre interaction. Hildegard spoke, and her tone had a hint of curiosity to it.

“I can't stand that woman, yet I am fascinated by her. She lives in a parallel world, where she thinks nothing can get to her because she is beautiful and popular.”

Steve spoke next, and they discussed it amongst each other.

“To some extent, it is true.”

"Is there anything we can do to keep her around, detective?"

"I don't think so. It is all circumstantial, we don't have anything to tie her to the murder."

"One thing she has in her favour."

"What is that, Mrs Hildegard?"

"She mentioned blood. As far as I'm aware, not many people outside this room know the condition the body was found. She might have done it deliberately, but that would be very curious if she did. I wonder if we will ever see her again, now that she is leaving the country."

"I wouldn't worry *too* much about it, we will probably know where she is the whole time just by looking at our phones. And Dubai extradites, so we could get her back very easily if we wanted."

"She mentioned Lebanese heritage, mate - I wonder if she is also a Lebanese citizen. One quick flight away and she'd be in her second home country, legally."

"I haven't thought about this. That would certainly complicate things. Time will tell."

"Time will tell. Looks like we should hear the secretary next, Mrs Anna Smith."

"She was already on my list, but now I will try and get her here today. Felicity, could you please call Mrs Smith and ask her to come in? Please ask if her husband would also like to join. Don't tell them they are subpoenaed, because they are not. But make it sound like they *have* to come, it would be beneficial and less suspicious for them to. You know what I mean."

Felicity knew what he meant, and went away to make some calls. Steve turned to Hildegard.

"Where the hell did you find that picture?"

But I was the one who answered.

"It was fixed on the board in Jack's home office, above the table with the laptop."

Steve looked *furious*. I could practically see the smoke starting to come off his ears, like in cartoons. He opened his mouth to scream, but Hildegard was faster.

"Now, now, detective. Before you start screaming and accusing me, I did not take anything away from the scene. I have been doing this long enough to know better. It's much simpler than that. I used this incredible device I have right here in my pocket, it's called a 'phone', and took a picture of the picture. After we left the scene, I popped into my office and asked my receptionist to have it printed for me. The original is still there, untouched, on the board. And I think it should stay there, at least for now."

That woman would not stop surprising me. I clearly remember her going to her office after we came back from the flat, while I stayed in to take my nap. I looked at her in awe, and she seemed to appreciate it. I also took another look at the picture, and now I knew who everyone was. Jack was standing on the left with Lily beside him, trying to hug him. She looked disgusted at the woman standing on her right, who now I assumed was Anna Smith. Anna hugged a man, presumably her husband Martin.

Beside them was Cedric Dupont, and at the right end of the picture stood Andrew. Somehow most of the suspects were gathered in this one picture, together. Well, except for Alisson Ling, who was nowhere to be seen in the shot.

Before we went out for lunch, Felicity came back and informed us that Mrs Anna Smith would come in for a statement the next morning, at nine AM, before her shift would start. In her own words, Mr Dupont graciously gave her the morning off. Felicity could not reach Mr Smith yet, but left him a message at his workplace. Dr Sanjay asked us if we could have a briefing at three o'clock in the afternoon, which would give us roughly one hour and fifteen minutes for lunch.

We had some food in a sandwich shop about a block away from the station, and I sat in front of the sea with a bar of chocolate for fifteen minutes. It was the first day without wind, and although still very cold, the sun shone and the sea looked like a lake - no waves to be seen. It was the perfect opportunity for me to enjoy the beautiful coastline of the south of England. I was on my own, but I enjoyed that moment of solitude by the sea. All things considered, times like this gave me hope about living in Brighton for the future.

At three we were all back in the station, and Dr Sanjay started his briefing.

“First of all, the toxicology report is not ready yet. I apologise. They are very busy at the lab, with all the people away on holiday, lots of sickness, and they are handling all the tests in Sussex and some of Kent and Surrey. But they said it should be in our hands tomorrow afternoon.”

“That should be ok, we still have some people to question.”

“I asked the Marina Management for all the footage they could provide of the day of the crime, but I have yet to receive an answer from them.”

Hildegard grinned and spoke, her tone was of someone who was about to tell a joke.

“Good luck with that. There will be no footage.”

“I wouldn’t be so sure, that place is akin to a closed community and they have cameras everywhere.”

"They do, but those cameras were not working that day. In fact, I believe they are back online today."

"How can you be so sure?"

"There was a notice from the Marina Management on the board above Jack's laptop, in his office, saying that they are upgrading the system and that the CCTV would be turned off between the thirty first of December and the fourth of January."

I remembered seeing that note, but I confess that I did not pay attention to its content at the time. I was so eager to get to the living room that everything else seemed unimportant. Steve hit his left fist down the table.

"Ah, damn it! I was hoping to see who came in and out of that flat. Lucky bugger."

"Maybe. Maybe they chose that date knowingly. The management is required to make those notices public, besides of course sending them to the residents, so that note can be seen in its website. It had been issued on the tenth of December, plenty of time. I went to the website to look for it myself. I was wondering if the killer had seen it on Jack's board instead. But it might not be the case."

Dr Sanjay looked disappointed, but he continued in his usual documentary-narrator-style voice.

"Anyway, I chased any possible CCTV footage available around your office. The closest one is at the Pavilion. I mean, the closest one in the direction of the Marina, as the Train Station also has CCTV available. But there are no trains to/from the Marina, and a preliminary look at the Pavilion footage seems to confirm Jack walked to your office. I wasn't able to find any footage of him walking back, but I assume he took an uber or a taxi home, seeing as he was in a hurry to meet someone - according to the statement from Miss Hughes."

I was hopeful this could have been traced, and I expressed that.

"It shouldn't be difficult to trace that uber or taxi, right?"

Dr Sanjay answered.

"Well, actually, it depends. If he took an uber, it should be very straightforward - the app registers all trips. If he took a taxi, things get a bit more complicated. We would have to chase all the taxi companies, if he called for one or if he got one straight off the street, ask drivers, check which ones have CCTV installed in their cars; and if he paid in cash, it would be even harder to pin down. It would be like searching for a needle in a haystack."

Hildegard made another one of her enigmatic observations.

"I am willing to bet he did not take an uber."

Steve looked irritated.

"How can you be so sure of that?"

"Through the simple power of observation, detective: he did not have any phone with him, while he was in the office waiting for me. We all saw that footage. He sat down for half an hour without a phone. I cannot see why he would keep his phone hidden away for half an hour while sitting and waiting, something we can all agree would be very boring for a young man; And then magically produce said phone to hire an uber the minute he left the office. Maybe he forgot his phone at home?

I'm sure it happened to us all. I would even go further and suggest he paid in cash, just to make our lives harder now."

She laughed, and that broke the tension. Dr Sanjay concluded his short briefing.

"There is not much more to say, then. I was hoping I would be able to offer some hope on a future update about the footage from the Marina, but that's a dead end now. Apart from the toxicology reports, there is not much more we can do and we have to rely on the statements. I have officers checking the alibis we currently have, and I will update you all as soon as I hear something. For now, let's plan another briefing tomorrow afternoon, with the results from the lab."

Steve took the lead.

"Sounds good to me, doctor. Felicity, I need to have a chat with you about some tasks and documents, but this shouldn't take long. The rest of you, I will see you back here tomorrow at a quarter to nine?"

We said our goodbyes and left. Hildegard went to her office, as she hadn't been in much for the past few days and had to take care of some things. I accompanied her to her office building, because I wanted to take a walk in the city and get to know a bit of the area. When we got to her building, she went in, I said hi to Miss Hughes and continued on my way. Not before noticing how the receptionist looked puzzled, being greeted by name by someone she didn't know.

I walked around the Laines, entered some shops here and there, but did not buy anything. One caught my attention for the amazing smell of sweet butter: they were making their own fudge, there and then. There were also many cafes and stores that did not seem to belong to any chain or franchise, this place was a paradise for independent business. I passed in front of a bakery that showed delicious things for sale, walked towards the library and stopped in front of a cafe inside a place called The Ledward Centre. The atmosphere looked very welcoming, lively, and the people inside talked to each other and smiled. But maybe most importantly, it looked warm inside, so I entered and had a lovely cup of herbal tea, while chatting to one of their volunteers. He was wearing a beanie cap shaped like a panda, which made me giggle every time I looked at it.

On my way home I did some grocery shopping and, as I had some time that evening, I decided to cook something for myself. I thought about the evenings with my colleagues, when we cooked together between reviews for tests, and how I really missed them. I checked our text chain group, saw the memes and gifs, and told everyone I missed them. About ten minutes later we were in a group video call with way too many people to be able to get a word in, but I felt home. For the first time in Brighton, I felt home. I felt surrounded by people I loved, even if virtually. I invited them to come over at some point, and they all promised to do it. We finished the call and I went to sleep feeling great. That night, I had the best night's sleep since I arrived in Brighton.

Chapter Eight

Let me get this straight

I woke up on that Thursday morning around seven-thirty AM. As always, I made myself a cup of coffee and a bowl of porridge and sat in front of the TV, fully expecting all news to be about the investigation. I tried to look for something other than news, but nothing seemed very interesting. I swapped through channels until I saw a face I have seen before - three times now. It was a picture of Cedric Dupont, and the voice over said 'Today, at ten-thirty we will have a special guest. Mr Cedric Dupont, from Honeywell-Dupont, will be in the studio to talk to us about the future of his law firm and give us insights in the investigation of the death of Jack Honeywell. Right after the business brief at ten.'

I got my phone to call Hildegard, but I stopped myself from doing so. I would see all of them soon, it was nice to enjoy my breakfast away from it all for a bit longer. I had a nice shower and got myself ready. At eight-thirty, I walked in the direction of the station. The street was not as packed as it had been the day before. There were still cars from the news stations, but with fewer reporters and no equipment to show live transmissions. There were also less onlookers. Traffic had been reestablished in the street, and it was not very difficult to get into the building.

I entered the room at exactly a quarter to nine and everyone was already inside. I started by delivering the news of what I saw earlier.

"Good morning, everyone! I guess we all know why Mr Dupont graciously gave Mrs Smith the morning off..."

For the first time, I felt like I was delivering news that nobody knew. Steve questioned me about it.

"What on earth are you talking about?"

"He will be interviewed today at ten-thirty about the future of his law firm with Lord Honeywell."

"Oh, really? That is an interview we do not want to miss. Felicity invited him to an interview, but I don't think he is coming."

Felicity then spoke. She didn't really talk much about investigation things, which made me pay extra attention to it.

"He said he *would* be willing to give a statement, but asked to see *everything* we had gathered so far. Reports, other statements, all the information I could give him, so he could prepare his statement."

"Kinda defeats the purpose. I guess we don't want a planned statement."

Steve started talking again.

"You're damn right, kid, we don't. But if we put him under caution, he has the right to see what we have against him. And he knows that. Let's see what he is willing to share with the media later. Here comes Mrs Smith."

Mrs Anna Smith was a tiny woman - I would have been surprised if she was taller than five feet. She looked exactly like a secretary from an old black and white movie: light brown hair, pulled together and tucked in above her head in a donut, hazel eyes, light makeup and thin round glasses. She was dressed in a mustard pantsuit and wore high hill shoes. Her voice had the efficient tone of a secretary, and she spoke very standard English, with a very standard accent. Talking to her was like watching the news.

"Good morning, Mrs Smith. Thank you for accepting our invitation."

"Good Morning, detective. It is my pleasure to help."

"My name is Stephen Pritchard, I am the Lead Investigator in the investigation into the death of Jack Honeywell. This is a voluntary interview and it is being recorded in writing by Felicity Browne-Porter, Assistant Investigator. You are not considered a suspect at this point, but we are treating everyone involved in this case as a person of interest. Therefore, I am putting you under caution. This means you can end this interview anytime and you do not have to say anything. However, it may harm your defence if you do not mention when questioned something which you later rely on in court. Anything you do say may be given in evidence. You will have a chance to read and sign a copy of the transcript of your interview once it is over. Finally, I would like to remind you that you have the right to legal representation before proceeding. Do you understand and agree to start?"

"Perfectly. I understand and I agree."

"Thank you. I want to start with the interview Mr Dupont is giving today. Were you aware of it?"

"As his secretary, I made the arrangements for the interview. I hope that answers your question."

"Do you know what he will say?"

"I am afraid I don't. But I believe he will talk about the future of the business."

"Do you know what will be the future of the business?"

"I believe Monsieur Dupont wants to continue their law practice. I know for a fact Lord Honeywell was against it. But I believe Andrew gave him the green light to proceed, now that Jack passed away."

“Did you hear this conversation between Andrew and Mr Dupont?”

“No, I did not. But Monsieur Dupont made a comment about it - that is where I got this information.”

“Do you know why Lord Honeywell did not want the practice to continue after his death?”

“I do not, I am afraid. But I know that Monsieur Dupont has been adamant about it. He tried to convince Jack, who was also against it, at our office Christmas party, about two weeks ago. Things escalated between them two.”

“Could you please elaborate?”

“Monsieur Dupont tried to talk to Jack about it, but Jack would not agree. Monsieur Dupont had been drinking and became very agitated, and at one point he said that he would do whatever it took to keep the business going. If that meant destroying the people in his path, so be it.”

“Did he? That is most interesting. Did anyone else hear this argument?”

"Yes. Everyone at the party could hear it, he was not discreet about it. He was inebriated and quite altered. Andrew intervened and separated them. He took Monsieur Dupont aside, and I did not see either of them again."

"Have you always worked for Mr Dupont?"

"No, I used to work for Lord Honeywell. Monsieur Dupont was something like a consulting lawyer, he did not really work the cases directly. He would deal with the less important parts, like attending court appointments of witnesses, depositions, mediations... As part of my work for Lord Honeywell, I would support Monsieur Dupont, but that did not take much of my time. When Lord Honeywell retired, Monsieur Dupont took over, and I became his secretary. But it hasn't been the same."

"What do you mean?"

"There are no new cases at the moment. We are dealing with ongoing cases, the ones we already took. But we haven't gotten any new cases since Lord Honeywell left."

"Is there a reason for that?"

"Lord Honeywell is the star of the team. And the company always reached out, they never took walk-ins. I would say the uncertainty has prevented Monsieur Dupont from doing so, but this is only a supposition from my side. And it is one of the reasons Monsieur Dupont wants to change their business model, so he would have more chances to act and to get out of someone else's shadow . He wanted to take in cases that reached out to them, not only the ones they chose to defend. He had tried to do it for years, but his partner was against it. After his partner retired, Monsieur Dupont saw it as the perfect opportunity to make the change."

"Mr Dupont has been here and was asked to give a volunteer statement, just like you are doing now, but he refused, alleging that he had a client waiting for him. I believe he called you to confirm. Is that true, did he really have a client waiting for him?"

"I am not at liberty to discuss that question, because it might involve client/attorney privilege."

"I understand. There is something else I would like to discuss with you, something of a more *delicate* matter. There was a rumour that you and Jack were romantically involved. Is that true?"

"I was expecting to be asked about that, and I would like to use this opportunity to set the record straight: Jack and I were *only friends*, nothing else. I offered him support when he was going through something very difficult in his life, something I would rather not discuss before you ask me, and we became very close. But there was nothing more than an innocent friendship."

"How did your husband react to that?"

Her facial expression changed, she looked a bit more relaxed and her manner became slightly less formal.

"Martin is a caveman. It was extremely appealing when I met him, but I was a different person then. I evolved in the world, he didn't. Naturally he was upset about the whole thing. He threatened Jack at the christmas party, saying that he would show him what happened to someone who messed with his wife. I took him aside and scolded him for embarrassing me in front of everyone I worked with. I also told him that there was nothing between Jack and me and, most importantly, I was not his property. But he is my husband, and I love him, so I wanted to make it work."

"Did this feud between them escalate any further after the party?"

"Quite the opposite! Jack very graciously paid for our holiday in the Maldives. It was a way to get us back together, reconnect. I thought I could show Martin some class, get him to be less monster and more prince. Jack was very thankful for all the support I gave him, he said the holiday was the least he could do for me. Martin seems to have understood afterwards that we were just friends. Especially after Jack passed away. And I have to be honest, it was nice to have my husband feel jealous about me. In a way, it spiced up our relationship. Jack would have been happy about it, I am sure. He wanted the best for us, and the feeling was mutual."

"Did you ever suspect your husband to be involved in Jack's death?"

"Absolutely not. Martin barks a lot, but he would never do such a thing. I am sure of it. Besides, he was either at work or with me that day."

"Right, let's talk about your whereabouts, but let's start with the Maldives. When were you two there?"

"We went there for Christmas and New Year's, between the twenty third of December and the first of January, when we landed back. I had to work on the second."

"Could you please recount your whereabouts on the second of January then?"

"Certainly. I went to work in the morning, at nine AM. I had my lunch break in the building, we have a terrace with a beautiful view of the Downs, and I left around a quarter to five. Martin picked me up and we drove to Lewes for a dinner date. We were home around seven thirty."

"Could you tell me the name of the restaurant where you had your date?"

"We ended up not going to a restaurant. We bought some groceries and drove to the Seven Sisters, close to Eastbourne. It was a beautiful evening, we parked the car close to the cliffs and enjoyed the view."

"It was very cold to be outside."

"Yes, but we blankets and lit a small fire. It was very romantic, under the stars."

"Was there anyone else with you? Anyone who could corroborate your story?"

"No, it was just us two. I suppose it would not have been very romantic if someone else was there."

"I understand. Is there anything else you would like to tell us at this stage?"

"Nothing comes to my mind."

Steve did not have any more questions, so he concluded the interview and advised her that she wasn't under caution anymore. Felicity printed the statement, Mrs Smith read it, signed it and handed it back. Before she left, Steve asked her whether she knew if her husband was coming for a statement.

"I don't know, detective. Martin is a very busy man. I will ask him when I see him."

She left, and Hildegard made some comments.

"I would be very surprised if Mr Smith showed his face. I am also wondering what is the thing she supported Jack with."

"The death of his mother? The fact that his father had terminal cancer and would probably die soon?"

"We all know these things, detective. They are public. She could have told them, she would not have been indiscreet by doing so. Instead, she said it was something she would rather not discuss with us. No, I am inclined to think it is something else. Something we don't know."

That left us all thinking, but it did not last long. Shortly after, Felicity came into the room and told us that the TV was ready for us to watch Mr Dupont's interview. Mr Dupont was a short bald man and had a moustache. He was wearing a dark brown suit with a mahogany tie. On the left side of his chest he wore a black ribbon. His french accent was almost imperceptible when he spoke. But first, the host introduced the segment.

"Good morning and welcome to 'The Stakeholder'! Today we will be talking to Monsieur Cedric Dupont, from the Honeywell-Dupont law firm. His partner, Lord Honeywell, is now retired and in treatment for a medical condition, and the name Honeywell was back in the news after the death of his only son, Jack. The police are currently investigating the death, and I believe it is being currently treated as under suspicious conditions. Is that right Monsieur Dupont?"

"Good morning, and thank you for having me. It is a pleasure to be here. Yes, you are correct, the death is currently being investigated and we are offering the police all the support we can. In fact, we are being kept in close contact with the detectives responsible for the investigation."

"Is there anything you can tell us about the developments in the case?"

"Unfortunately, I cannot disclose any information at this point. That could be prejudicial for the investigation."

"But is there a suspect in mind? Do you think an arrest is going to be made soon?"

"There are some suspects being questioned right now, and I have trust in the police. I believe it won't be long until something significant happens."

"Your law firm is known for offering defence to the most indefensible cases. Are you planning on offering your services to the accused murderer of Mr Jack Honeywell?"

"Well, first of all, as I said before, his death is still being investigated. It is too early to talk about murder. Secondly, I think there would be a conflict of interest there, which might not be beneficial for the accused. But we will look into it when it comes to that. For now, we are sitting with the police and being at their disposal, to support them however we can."

"There are rumours that Lord Honeywell would not want the practice to continue under his name. Are those rumours true?"

"Absolutely not, Lord Honeywell and I built this company and our exceptional reputation, and I cannot see why he would want to throw this away after so many years. Besides, I have the full support of his kids to continue acting without their father. Jack supported me before, and Andrew supports me now."

"So Honeywell-Dupont is open for business?"

"We are. In fact, we are changing our business model: we will be accepting walk-ins now. We will be analysing every case individually, but we wanted to open ourselves for the wider public, to give everyone a chance to have a fair defence."

"That is an interesting development. I have one last question for you, Monsieur. In your professional opinion, do you think Jack Honeywell was murdered?"

"I think it is a possibility, yes. But it is too early to say. I say: let the police do their job. I can assure you that we will have an answer soon."

"Thank you very much for being here! That was Monsieur Cedric Dupont, from Honeywell-Dupont, saying they are open for business. And for us, it is business as usual. The government is changing the interest rate for the third time in six months. We will be right back with this and other business news to start your day. Stick around!"

Steve looked infuriated. I think it was the first time I heard him curse.

"What a fucking nutcase. Helping the police? He did not do a bloody thing for us."

Hildegard tried to calm him.

"Well, at least we got a sort of statement, and it confirms what Mrs Smith said. I think it is odd, though, that he said he had the support from the whole family, when we all heard her saying he does not. Of course, he cannot be fact-checked when it comes to Jack or his father."

We went back into our usual room and started to prepare to go for lunch. Steve informed us he would be out that afternoon, and would not be back until the next morning. He had to attend something related to another case. Dr Sanjay did not receive the toxicology reports yet, so he would not be giving us a briefing that day. Hildegard said she would stick around after lunch and take a look at everything we had so far from the investigations. She also wanted to catch up properly with Felicity.

I stayed for the survey of the investigation files, and we discussed some things that had been said, most of them the points that Hildegard had already raised before. When Hildegard joined Felicity for their catch up, I left. I enjoyed having some time free, as an old friend would be in Brighton that night and we would have dinner together. It was nice to see a familiar face, talk about old times and what we had been up to. I talked about working in the investigation, but did not give too many details. I thought it would be improper of me to do so, and my friend understood.

Friday morning was a late one for me. I was not aware of anything planned in the station that morning, and I received no call from anyone. I slept a bit later, took my time in the morning and arrived at the station close to eleven AM. When I got to our room, the door was closed. I had not even registered that there was a door there, as I had never seen it closed. Hildegard and

Felicity were also outside. From inside, a loud voice sounded very irritated. When I arrived, the conversation was already halfway through.

"...For god's sake, man! The press is breathing down my neck! Today I got a call from the Home Secretary! *The bloody Home Secretary!* These people, they are well connected. Something needs to be done, we need to arrest someone!"

"Commissioner, you know very well that I cannot declare this a murder until I have the report. And until I declare it a murder, I cannot do much to keep these people around. My hands are tied."

"Greece! One of our suspects is in bloody Greece! Do you understand the headache it will be to get her back here!"

"I do, ma'am. But as I said, I cannot do anything until we are sure."

"I don't care! I want something done! Look at this piece of garbage. How did they get this? Why don't we know about it?

How do you think it makes me look when people get the news from this rubbish of a newspaper instead of us?"

"I will ask the doctor to chase the report again."

"Don't bother! I called them and told them to stop everything else and get this done. You should have it this afternoon."

"Thank you ma'am."

"Steve, arrest someone. If we are wrong, we will deal with it later."

"You know I cannot do that."

"Yes, I know."

Then the door opened, and the commissioner left without acknowledging any of us. Steve looked like a dog who had just been told off by his owner. We came in, and I saw the newspaper on top of the desk. It was showing a picture of Jack.

'Exclusive! Jackie Oh! The secret life of the devil's heir.'

Under his picture, a smaller text was written.

'The apple does not fall far from the tree. A neighbour tells us all details about his secret life: parties, late night visits and sketchy businesses. All the gossip on page three!'

It was an article written with information received from an unidentified neighbour, although I had a very good idea of who it was. There were all sorts of stories about Jack having sex parties with multiple people, being visited by strange men and women at the late hours of the night and it insinuated that his flat was the front for an illegal operation for smuggling and contraband of things like fake perfumes, counterfeit cigarettes and adulterated alcohol. But the paper was careful enough to use words such as 'alleged' and 'according to the neighbour', probably in order to exempt themselves from any liability.

We were all shocked with the article, but the bad news did not stop there. Felicity explained that Alisson Ling had left the country, the commissioner was referring to her when she talked about Greece. I thought I knew how she managed to do it.

"She probably got a considerable sum of money for her story. Those tabloids pay good money for a headline. It doesn't surprise me."

Hildegard was reflective, and when she spoke, it felt like she was choosing the words.

"It is no doubt an interesting hypothesis. But it makes me wonder why she would say some of the things she did. It doesn't really fit with the idea I have about her."

Steve was still silent. When he spoke, his voice did not have any assurance.

"This is bad."

I never saw Steve so deflated like that. He looked lost. Nobody spoke for a while, and he was the one to break the silence once again.

"I gotta get something to eat. I'll be back this afternoon."

We also went to get lunch, and we were back around one-thirty PM. Steve was sitting, reflective. We greeted him, but he did not look up. A few minutes after we arrived, Dr Sanjay came into the room holding a piece of paper. Steve jumped off his seat.

“Sanjay, please tell me you have the report!”

“Steve, methanol poisoning. In the body, in the glass, in the stain. This was murder.”

Steve hit his left fist down the table and celebrated. Apparently he did it when he was angry and when he was happy. Cursing seemed to go the same way.

“Fucking hell! Now I can do something! Felicity, get the paperwork. We've got stuff to do!”

For the next hour, we were involved with the documentations and procedures related to a murder investigation. Felicity was showing me how things were done, what needed to be filled, where to dispatch them to, all the things that happen behind the scenes to make the police work legal. I have seen most of it in the academy, and I was happy to be able to put it all into practice.

Steve asked Felicity to call Mr Dupont and Mr Smith for a statement, but both men refused when they were informed that this was now the part of a murder investigation. They said they would need to be summoned if they were a suspect, and they would come with their lawyers, should that be the case. Steve said he could arrange that, but the fact that this was Friday afternoon did not help.

Around four PM Andrew came in. He was holding a copy of the newspaper article.

"Have you seen this atrocity? Dad is fuming. He said he cannot believe she *actually* went through with it. I believe the exact words he used were 'evil bitch'. I have never seen him so angry. No, I lie, he was also very angry yesterday, when we watched the interview uncle Cedric gave on TV."

Hildegard began a conversation with him.

"How is your uncle, Andrew?"

"Dad is not well. To have to see all this, must be horrible for him. At least his mind is not what it used to be anymore, so I'd say silver linings?"

It always got me how Andrew had the tendency of saying the wrong things at the wrong times. He was not very good at reading the room, and although it was intended as humour, probably to deflect everything that he had to go through, it came across as a bit distasteful. Hildegard didn't seem to mind.

"It must not be easy, I agree with you."

"By the way, Mrs Hildegard, dad would like to see you. He is very keen to talk to you. Could you please come to the house tomorrow, at lunchtime?"

"To see me? Do you know why?"

"He wouldn't say. He only said it was imperative he would finally meet you in person before he died, and he assumes you wouldn't want to deny a dying man his wish. I hate when he talks like that."

"By all means, he is absolutely right, I would never decline his invitation. It will be my pleasure to come and see him tomorrow."

She wrote down the address and he turned around to leave.

"You will have to excuse me, but I have to go. I have a date tonight."

The idea of Andrew dating someone was something that *never* crossed my mind before. I wonder how many wrong things he would do and silly jokes he would tell before his date would get up and leave.

Chapter Nine

No parent should see their children die

That Saturday morning was sunny and beautiful. Maybe that was why people liked to live in Brighton: I had been here for a week, and there was no sign of rain. If this was the winter, I could not wait to see what the summer would be like. Granted, it had been cold the whole week, but we finally had temperatures approaching double digits. I planned to meet Hildegard in front of the police station at eleven AM, which gave me plenty of time to enjoy the sun at Queens Park. The park was a mere five minutes walk from my flat and I had to go up the hill, but it was worth it. It was full of people laying down, playing sports, playing with their children. It did not feel like the English winters I was used to.

We caught the bus to Hove around five minutes past eleven, travelled for about thirty five minutes and alighted in a beautiful street, in a higher part of town, with big mansions and no flat buildings to be seen. We walked up the street looking at the house numbers, trying to identify number sixty-three. We spotted it on the side of one of the houses, crossed the garden between the street and the entrance and knocked on the door.

We were greeted by a governess dressed as one would expect a governess from those nineties sitcoms to be dressed. Hildegard told her who we were and why we were there. As soon as we entered the house it was clear to me we had stepped into a different world. It was a proper mansion, one I would have never expected to see in Hove.

The hall was beautifully decorated with paintings and sculptures, opening to other areas of the house. On the left was an open plan living room, and I could see two sets of sofas and a relaxing chair in between them, a centre table and what looked like a persian rug. There was no TV, but a fireplace had ashes, probably the remains of the fire lit the night before. The room was also decorated with paintings and vases. To the right of the hall, there was a door slightly open, leading to something that looked like a library. In front of us, there was a beautiful marbled staircase, and on each side of it there were doors, both of them closed.

The governess took us upstairs, where a large corridor led to at least 5 doors, all of them closed. The corridor seemed to follow the same decoration pattern as the other parts of the house I saw. She knocked in one of the doors and a man answered. Based on the way he was dressed, I guessed he was the nurse in charge of Lord Honeywell. The governess introduced ourselves to the nurse.

“Thank you very much, Dolores. Hi, please, do come in. I am nurse Muller, we have been waiting for you. It has been a busy week, but we are almost ready to enjoy the weekend now. There is one more person he wants to see after you leave. But I don't know how much he can do in one day.”

As soon as we entered, I noticed how the room had clearly been changed, adapted to accommodate a sick person’s new needs. It might have been an office, maybe a bedroom, but it now looked like a hospital room, with equipments, medicine flasks. A small sink and basin had been installed in one of the corners. On the far side of the room a window was open, and it was possible to spot the sea in the distance, and the city of Hove in between. The midday sun shone golden, making the landscape even prettier. There was a regular, queen size bed, not a hospital one, which made the room feel more homely. In the desk right beside the bed there were many pictures in beautiful frames. Some of them were of the family, others I could not identify the people. The man we came to see was sitting at a chair by the window.

Nurse Muller called his patient's attention.

"Milord, Mrs Hildegard and her associate are here."

Lord James Honeywell was an older version of Jack and, to some extent, Andrew. He had blue-green eyes, was clean shaven, but the light freckles and the ginger blond turned white hair showed its similarities with the young ones. He looked very debilitated, which was contrasting with the person we all knew from the media. He was gazing at the sea in the distance and did not speak for a while. When he did, his voice was weak, but firm.

"This is funny, this life. I finally get to see it all with clarity, and I won't be able to use any of it anymore. We are ephemeral, we are. Everything goes."

Hildegard did not seem to want to rush him. She spoke calmly and with patience, as if we could sit there for hours.

"I understand you wanted to see me, Milord."

"Yes, I did. Thank you for coming. For years I respected you, Mrs Hildegard. You put away the people that I looked for, and you did such a good job, that it took me much hard work to undo what you've done. You were my arch enemy, my kryptonite, my chess opponent. And now, here we are, sitting together, trying to walk the same path. Life is funny."

"I am flattered to have your respect, sir."

"I would be defending this person! You know that, right? I would be the lawyer who would pick their case. I would be defending the one who murdered my poor Jack. I probably defended the murderers of many different Jacks in my day.

Maybe everyone is right, maybe I do deserve everything that I got in life."

"Everyone has a choice."

"It's not that simple, not as black and white. I would expect you to know that by now. Sometimes we have to make certain choices for the bigger picture, sometimes we have to choose the least worst outcome. I learned this the hard way."

He fell silent and his eyes seemed to lose focus. Hildegard remained silent. The nurse spoke in a whisper tone.

"He is taking really heavy medication, you see. He is not always himself. Sometimes, his mind goes."

"Does he understand that Jack is dead?"

"There's a perfect word in German to answer this: Jain - 'ja' and 'nein', merged together. Sometimes it is very clear that he is aware of everything, sometimes he still talks about Jack as if he is still alive. It's been like that for a while. About a month ago, he had a full conversation with Andrew thinking it was Jack. Bless him, Andrew, patiently went along with it as if nothing was out of order."

The mention of both names seemed to bring Lord Honeywell out of his trance.

"Jack and Andrew, my boys. Some people are very unfortunate. They are put in this world together with horrible people, through no fault of their own. They are just born in the wrong place. Don't listen to what other people tell you, those two love each other. They are brothers. They grew up like brothers, having the kind of fun brothers have. They tricked their teachers, they fought for girls, they pretended to be twins to get in and out of trouble. Jack and Andrew, what an unusual and unexpected connection. They are both amazing boys, who turned into fine men, despite being born in the wrong place, with the wrong people. I know what that is, I know what it is to have a brother. I was not as lucky as they are, but I definitely know what it is to be in the wrong place, with the wrong people."

"Why do you say so?"

"My late brother John, may the lord have mercy on his soul, he was not a good man. He came from the factory missing something, something that could not be fixed. He was not fit for this world, and although I felt his passing with the pain of a brother, I knew this was better in the grand scheme of things. His wife chose to follow him, and I could not stop her. She also did not have anything to do with any of this, she was also in the wrong place, and paid the price for it. Remarkable woman, she was. Played her part of the good wife until the end, even though he made her life miserable for that one mistake. I will forever admire her."

He stopped, as if he could not speak anymore. But he did, and he sounded defiant.

"But I had to do what I had to do to make the world a better place for everyone else. And the world did become a better place without him. Sadly she became a collateral. I resented that. Remarkable woman."

"Are you trying to tell me that you..."

"It is all buried, all in the past. Some ghosts are better kept under the white sheets. Revealing them would do nobody no good, I know that well now. There is no need to talk about this again, repeat myself. We all have to make choices, and deal with their consequences. I guess my way of dealing with it was to become the person I would have needed to rely on back then. I also took Andrew in, it was the obvious thing to do. The decent one too, I say. Considering..."

"How is he your nephew?"

"Is he though? Sarah knew, god rest her beautiful soul. She was like a mother to him, more than I was a father. Blood is not always thicker than water, as they say. She knew what she had to do. She always knew what to do. That's why we are all so lost without her. Especially Andrew. He and Sarah were connected in such a strong way, even though they never shared any blood ties. Life is funny."

"Were you not connected to Andrew?"

"Of course, of course. But Andrew reminded me of John, and everything that happened between us. There was too much guilt, too much baggage. John knew. Andrew, poor Andrew, punished for being born. Jack, on the other hand, he was my boy! The boy I always wanted to have. He had to be perfect, I did everything right. At least I thought I did. Maybe that's why my disappointment and resentment was so strong when he told me. I wanted a normal life, I wanted grandkids I could brag about to my friends. I couldn't understand it. We are afraid of things we don't understand. Nobody ever told me how to be ok with it."

"That's not an easy conversation to have, from either side."

"That's probably why he did it, it's why he killed himself. Because I couldn't understand. I failed him."

I spoke, once again faster than my mind could think.

"The police don't think that he killed himself."

Hildegard stopped me. Lord Honeywell did not seem to notice it.

"It's all the same, he is coming to meet me, he told me he will come meet me when it is all over. I will tell him I am ok with it. I love him just the way he is. I want him to be happy. I understand it now. None of that matters anymore, it's all in the past, and so will I be soon."

"Do you know if Jack told anyone else about this?"

Hildegard asked the last question, but he went back into his trance. She also fell silent, reflecting on what she had heard. Nurse Muller asked if we were intending to stay much longer - he worried that his patient was becoming overwhelmed, especially considering he still had someone else to see. We prepared to leave, but this seemed to have brought Lord Honeywell back.

"Don't go, not yet. I need you, Mrs Hildegard."

"What can I do for you, Milord?"

"Take care of Jack and Andrew, will you please? They are surrounded by lions, and if they let their guard down, the lions will all try and devour them. It's only a matter of who will get to them first. I am terrified to think about who it will be, and what they will do to my boys."

"I am afraid I am too late, sir."

"These people, they are all pure evil. *All of them.* They have to be. You cannot do what I do, you cannot be who I am, without surrounding yourself with the worst kind of people. I hired them, I brought them into my world, I showed them my family. I exposed my boys to people who would harm them."

"All of them, or anyone in particular?"

"Oh yes, there is one. In fact, I know who did it. I know who ended Jack's life, and who is going to end Andrew's as well."

"Who would that be?"

"Me. I did. I damaged them. Maybe I am not the one who is giving them the fatal blow, but I started this. It came from me. History always repeats itself. Once again, I managed to damage something I put my hand on. I hope my boys can forgive me for taking away their lives."

Hildegard did not say anything for a while. When she did, she uttered the same words I heard once before.

"Lord Honewell, do you want the truth to come out?"

"Some ghosts are better left under white sheets, Mrs Hildegard."

"I don't know if I can agree."

"I wouldn't expect you to. But I would like to ask for your forgiveness. I would like to die knowing that you forgave me, that you forgave all of us."

Hildegard spoke in a very kind and human tone, one I never heard her use before. It felt like she was talking to her own grandparents.

"No parent should live to see their own children die."

"You are a very wise woman. I hope you are equally as kind."

With that, we got up and left the room.

I know who did it

"How about that! He just told us *everything*. Blood, what a magnanimous bond. Loyal to his kids until the end. It all makes sense, it all fits perfectly. I cannot believe it took me so long to see it."

We were standing in the front hall, and I was still trying to process everything we heard, when Hildegard spoke those words. Her tone was of excitement, and her eyes shone like her brain was working at extra capacity. I was completely dumbfounded.

"You cannot possibly think that *he* killed Jack?"

Hildegard laughed. It was a genuine laugh, almost as if she was relieved, as if a weight had been lifted from her shoulders.

"Mate, that is impossible. The man had not left his house for months. No, this was not a murder confession. But there were clues in what he said, clues that, when put together with all we know so far, make it all fit. It just works. And it's brilliant. Our murderer was very, very clever."

"I think I missed something, 'cause I have no clue of what you are talking about."

"You need to look at all the facts, and put them in the right places. This is your jigsaw puzzle, and you now have all the pieces in front of you; all you need to do is produce the picture. Ok, maybe you don't have *all* the pieces, there are still a few missing, but you should be able to infer them from context. Of course, we will need to test those hypotheses, but I am fairly certain they will work."

I was totally lost. So far, we heard many statements and analysis, and everyone seems to have dubious alibis that prevented them from committing the crime. Equally, everyone had motive, opportunity and means to kill Jack. Every single one of them - some more than others, for sure. Hildegard saw my confusion, and if her next statement was supposed to help, it did not.

"Start from the beginning. Think about it this way: what is the first thing we know about this case? When is the first thing *we* know about Jack Honeywell?"

"He was found dead?"

But Hildegard was not listening anymore. She was talking to the governess, who had just come in.

"Dolores, is Andrew in? I would like to have a quick word with him, before we leave."

"Certainly, Ma'am. Please take a seat in the living room, I will call him over."

It made sense. She probably wanted to assure him that the end was near, now that she knew who the killer was. We sat down, and almost immediately, Hildegard was on the phone.

"Hi, Felicity. Is detective Pritchard in? I need to talk to him. He is? Excellent. I should be there in about half an hour. Please tell him to wait for me. Yes, mate, I did! Don't tell him that, I need his help. Also, is your grandson still good with photoshop?

Good! I have something I would like him to do. I will explain everything to you when I am there. Ok, see you son, bye!"

I was even more confused than before. Steve? Why did she need to talk to Steve about anything? If she knew who the murderer was, why on earth did she have to ask Steve for help? At least I knew all my questions would have been answered soon, when we arrived at the station.

Andrew came into the living room about five minutes later.

"You wanted to see me, Mrs Hildegard."

"Yes, thank you for seeing me. This won't take long. I have some questions I would like to ask you about some of the people involved in this case. You don't need to answer them, if you don't want to. But if you do, I need you to promise to be completely honest."

"Sure."

"First of all, are you ok with Mr Dupont continuing to use the Honeywell name after your uncle passed away?"

"I haven't given it much thought, to be honest. I know Jack was against it, so was dad. In fact, dad was very cross with that interview uncle Cedric gave on TV, but I told you this already."

"Indeed you did. Do you think Mr Dupont would be a good lawyer to defend your cousin's murderer?"

"That would be a funny twist, wouldn't it? He wouldn't do such a good job, being so close to us. I don't think dad would allow it, anyway."

"Now, are you in love with Miss Ahmet?"

I don't think I have ever seen someone blush so quickly in their lives. Even I felt uncomfortable with the question, and I failed to see how this was anyway useful to anything. Andrew stuttered and answered the best way he could.

"Well... She is... A... Beautiful woman."

"That does not answer my question. Maybe I should rephrase it: If Miss Ahmet had chosen you instead of Jack, would you have dated her?"

"I... I suppose so."

“Was she the person you went on a date with yesterday evening?”

I swear that, if a shovel would magically appear right in front of us, Andrew would use it to dig a hole and bury himself in to hide away from this conversation. But he pulled himself together and once again, in the most Andrew way possible, answered.

“Yes. I asked her and she said yes. To be honest, I was surprised. I thought princesses only kissed frogs in fairy tales.”

“You told her about Jack’s alleged affair with Mrs Smith. Did you really see them together?”

“Let’s say I saw enough to know what was going on.”

“And was Mrs Smith worried about the reaction from her husband?”

“Funny enough, no. She said he would never do anything. She was very curious about how he found out about it.”

“Do you know how he found out about it?”

“No. But I swear I did not tell him.”

"Have you ever met Miss Alisson Ling?"

"No, I haven't. The closest I came from it was when I heard them arguing, but I never actually met her."

"Excellent. I only have one more question for you. Your cousin Jack, was he left handed or right handed?"

"Jack? He was left handed. It was our tell growing up."

"That is all the information I needed. Thank you for your honesty."

She gave him a wide smile that relaxed him, as if he got a sign that he was out of the spotlight. We said our goodbyes and left the house. She was walking very fast paced and seemed to be muttering things to herself. I couldn't find any chance to talk to her.

When we sat down inside the bus, I tried to ask Hildegard questions during the ride, but she insisted we did not talk about it. She would only answer "not here". I then tried asking other questions that had been on my mind since we left the room.

"Do you think Andrew will die too?"

"That depends. It's a difficult question, this one. I cannot answer it."

"He said that Jack killed himself. Could this really be suicide."

"No. But this was very revealing."

And she fell silent again. The bus ride did not take long. We walked the short distance between the stop and the police station. When we were about to enter, Hildegard stopped me. She looked truly sad and apologetic.

"I am very very sorry about this, I hope you will understand and forgive me: I need to have this conversation with detective Pritchard on my own, just the two of us. I must ask you to sit this one out."

Before I opened my mouth to protest, Hildegard started speaking again.

"I really wish I could bring you with me, I beg you to believe me. But we have a clever murderer on the loose, and so far they managed to elude all our efforts to understand this case. Until I am able to obtain all the proof I need to secure an arrest, but also a successful trial thereafter, I need to keep this a secret. I need the least amount of people to know this. It's not you, I will also ask Felicity not to participate in this meeting. It will be Steve and me, nobody else. Not even Dr Sanjay, at least not at this point."

"Why do you trust Steve and not me?"

"It is not a question of trust, mate. I can see why you would think that, but I need you to see things in a pragmatic perspective. Steve Pritchard is the lead investigator of this case, he is with the police. I could pop into places and ask them for reports, CCTV footage, but I am only a civilian. He has the actual power to get those things. I need to prove our killer was in certain places at certain times, doing certain things, and for that I need him. The truth needs him. Remember what I told Andrew when we started? I am working for the truth. That should be more important than anything, including the issues I have with the detective."

I hated the fact that everything she said made perfect sense. I wanted to plead my case, but against facts, there are no arguments. Hildegard saw that I understood, and gave me a hug. I was not expecting it, but it did make me feel better.

"You are an exceptional investigator. Just put the facts together, reflect on everything we saw, we heard, everything that happened so far. You've heard everything I've heard, you've seen everything I've seen. Every statement, every clue, every detail. Things even the other Investigators don't know. You have it all, you just need to put them in the right order. Start from the beginning and go. No theory is far-fetched. Test all the facts into the holes of the fabric, and stick to the ones that fit. The end is near. And, in the meantime, take some time off, get some rest. You deserve it."

I walked home but felt alone, more than I have ever felt since I arrived in Brighton. Hildegard became a friend, and now I felt abandoned without her. I did not know when I would see her again, and the prospect of a weekend on my own scared me. I decided to pack up my things and spend the weekend at my parents'. It would be good to eat mum's food, have a pint with dad, play with the dogs... It was a chance to recharge my batteries after this intense week.

My parents were thrilled to see me. Mum cooked my favourite food for dinner, dad bought my favourite beer. They tried not to ask me too many questions, and urged me to get some rest. Of course I heard all sorts of complaints that I was too thin, that I looked sick, that I wasn't eating right, that I did not call them enough. Parents are all the same, they just change their last name. That night I slept incredibly well. It was probably the best night sleep I had in months.

The next day, I woke up later than usual, around eleven forty-five in the morning. It was a wet and rainy Sunday morning, but not very cold. I missed the Brighton weather, but the rain was a nice sight in the countryside. My parents were out, probably doing some shopping or walking the dogs. I made myself a cup of coffee and turned on the TV. It was very cold outside, though the house was warm and cosy. I started passing the channels until I got to the news station. The headline on the screen brought me straight back into reality. "Breaking: Lord James Honeywell dead".

We had only seen him yesterday, yet it felt like an eternity. I thought about Andrew, and everything he went through in the last year. He lost his stepmother, with whom he was very attached. Then his step brother, with whom he grew up together. And now his step dad, the man who raised him. I could not even begin to fathom what was going through his head right now. I felt the urge to hug him, to tell him that all would be ok, that we were getting close to the end.

My thoughts were interrupted by a phone call. It was Hildegard.

"Mate, I assume you've seen it..."

"Yes, just saw the news. How awful for this family."

"I agree. But things are going in the right direction, and it won't be long until we reach the end."

"By the way, I didn't say anything, but I came to spend the weekend at my parents'. Is that ok?"

"That is the best thing you could have done. There is nothing here for you right now. Enjoy your time and replenish your energies, we have a full week ahead of us. But don't rush back, I don't expect things to start happening until Wednesday, at least. I will be away anyway, won't be back until Tuesday evening. Have a chat with the detective, he's officially your boss, but I would assume you don't need to be here before that. He's also been very busy. Anyway, talk soon. Bye!"

I hung up and called Steve, who told me it was ok for me to stay away until Wednesday morning. My parents arrived shortly after, and this time bombarded me with questions about the case. Now, with the news of Lord Honeywell dead, they wanted to know every detail of it. That name was once again dragged into every news report, every paper, online portal. The country did not talk about anything else.

The words Hildegard spoke to me, the last time we talked in person, echoed in my mind - how the less people who knew about it, the better it would be - so I lied to my parents. I told them I was not involved in this case, I was not senior enough to participate, and how everything was heavily guarded by the people involved in the investigation. I told them I only knew what was in the official bulletins sent out by the police, the same ones the press received. They seemed satisfied with my answer - after all, it made sense. It was surreal to think that I just arrived in Brighton for an internship and, the very next day, I became part of the biggest murder investigation the nation had seen in years. I would not have believed myself, had I not been there.

I decided to put my mind to work, and think about all the facts that I had, from the beginning. But my parents had other plans, so I set the investigator mindset aside and decided to enjoy my time with them. I would have enough time to get back into it, I had three more days ahead of me.

Then I blinked and it was Tuesday afternoon, gathering my things to get back to Brighton. I had spent the days doing all sorts of things that filled my time and my mind, hence why I had completely disconnected myself from everything that happened in the past week, and that had been good to me. I was not resenting coming back to Brighton as much as I thought I would be. It was good to know that I had a refuge, a place to go to be away from it all. But, strange as it sounds, I missed Brighton. I wanted to go back into the eye of the hurricane.

It did not feel like a hurricane, though. It was a very quiet Wednesday morning, when I got to the police station. The news cycle changed since the death of Lord Honeywell, and things were strangely quiet. Hildegard greeted me with a hug, which was very well received. She then updated me on what was going on.

"We have been doing investigations and gathering proofs, and so far nothing has contradicted my theory. It is all fitting perfectly, and we should have a case built within the next couple of days. Something else happened as well, something we are referring to as a happy accident. I do expect an arrest to happen until the end of the week."

"A happy accident? I am curious now! I completely turned myself off while I was away..."

"It's good that you did. In any case, you have a few more days to figure it out. Now, Lord Honeywell's death was ruled as a consequence of disease or health condition due to his illness, with no foul play involved. Everyone was happy with that, we all expected this outcome. In fact, there was proof to sustain it - a video clip. But I will circle back to that later. Anyway, he was cremated this morning. But, in an interesting twist, we were informed that Lord Honeywell was visited last week by Mr Dupont, Mrs Smith, Miss Ahmet, and the biggest surprise of them all: Miss Ling."

"Videotape? Visits? Miss Ling talking to Lord Honeywell? Wow, so much happened. I did not see any of that coming."

"Neither did I, but I have a good idea now why she went there. And remember how nurse Muller said he had another appointment after seeing us? He sat down with his attorney after we left and changed his will. Muller and Dolores were his witnesses. His previous will would basically leave everything to Andrew and Jack, but the new will was sealed and won't be opened until after his memorial. That was by his own wish."

"I wonder what will be in this new will."

"We are all wondering that. Nurse Muller is coming tomorrow to make a statement, and apparently there are some revelations awaiting us. It should keep us busy until the memorial Friday.

Oh yes, there is a small memorial service Friday at eleven AM at the family house in Hove, which was originally planned for Jack, but now will be held for both Jack and his father. This will be a small one, for family and close friends, whilst a bigger one, for important and famous people, is being planned in London later in the month."

"Looks like we will be busy."

But that day did not seem to be going very busily. Steve came in for a little bit around lunchtime, he told me the same things I heard from Hildegard earlier, but with a little more technical details. He seemed to be in a good mood, and was talking to me in a more kind and less condescending tone. He also seemed extremely busy, but not stressed.

I spent the rest of the day going through the investigation files, statements, crime scene pictures and reports. I was trying to find anything I had missed, but I could not see anything that would point me in any specific direction. It was perfectly possible that all of them murdered Jack. Maybe they all did? I remember a book I read where all the suspects killed the victim, together.

I went home that night, had some light dinner and went to bed relatively early. I was very excited to hear what nurse Muller would have to say. Maybe he would shine a light on the matter for me? I woke up the following day, did my usual coffee, porridge and TV routine, but the news was much the same, which is why it did not take me long to leave the house and head to the police station. I arrived around a quarter to nine, and everyone was in already. Nurse Muller was supposed to come at nine. And he was very punctual.

He sat down and Steve started the questioning, with the same thing he always said first.

"Mr Peter Muller, you have been invited to provide a statement as part of the ongoing investigation of the murder of Jack Honeywell. My name is Stephen Pritchard, I am the Lead Investigator in the investigation into the death of Jack Honeywell. This is a voluntary interview and it is being recorded in writing by Felicity Browne-Porter, Assistant Investigator. You are not considered a suspect, but we are currently building a case against an actual suspect, and we might need to use the contents of this interview in the process. You are not under caution and therefore not obliged to answer any questions, but everything you say could be admissible in a court of law. Do you understand and agree to proceed?"

"I do."

"Alright. I want to start with the visits. Who came to visit Lord Honeywell?"

"As I have previously said, we had visits from Monsieur Dupont, Mrs Smith and her husband, Miss Ahmet and Miss Ling. Of course, those are the people he didn't see on a normal basis, such as myself, Dolores, nurse Piotrowka - his night nurse - and Andrew. The rest of the staff would not come into the room as much, as his doctor thought it better to have less movement around him."

"Of course. When did the visits come?"

"Monsieur Dupont came on Tuesday, the third of January, in the late afternoon, with Andrew. First they showed him the press release about Jack's death, then Andrew and I left and they had their meeting. Miss Ahmet came on the afternoon of Wednesday, the fourth. Miss Ling came in later, in the evening. Mr and Mrs Smith came on Thursday, the fifth. We did not have any visits on Friday. Then Mrs Hildegard and her associate came Saturday, the seventh. Later that Saturday Lord Honeywell received his family attorney and changed his will. He passed away in the early hours of Sunday, the eighth of January."

"What was the content of those meetings?"

"Unfortunately I cannot give you that information."

"This is a murder investigation, it could certainly offer us some help..."

"It is not that, detective. I was not present to any of those meetings, so I don't know what they talked to each other about."

"Ah ok, I understand. Do you at least know anything about the content of the new will?"

"All I am allowed to tell you is that it's not to be opened until after the memorial service tomorrow. He also included a letter that is to remain sealed until after the murderer of Jack is found. If the murderer is never found, the letter is to remain sealed for fifty years."

"I think we will see this letter much earlier than that. And what about the video footage that was handed to the police? Did Lord Honeywell have the habit of filming things?"

"No, not really. There were some other videos, but that is the one I believed to be relevant to hand the police. The one that, according to him, would exonerate us all from any liability in his death. This was handed to the police already."

"Ah, yes, that is correct. Could you please describe that once again, explaining the thought process behind it?"

"Lord Honeywell was taking powerful opioids that had an effect on how his mind worked, making him prone to things like hallucinations and dissociation from reality, for example. He would have his medication administered every twelve hours, usually around six in the morning and six in the evening. It was also the time I started and finished work, exchanging with nurse

Piotrowka. About half an hour before his medication was administered, his mind was in its sharpest state, probably because the dosage was starting to wane off. Of course, there was a constant amount of drugs in his system and it would have taken days for it to wear off completely, but in comparison to the rest of the day, this was the time he would have a clearer view of the world around him."

"It makes sense."

"On the third, approaching the end of my shift, after Andrew informed his father that Jack had passed away, Lord Honeywell called Dolores, nurse Piotrowka, who had come in earlier following his request, and myself into the room, asked which one of us had the phone with the best camera, this was me, and he asked me to then put it on the table and film him talking to us. He told us it was his wish to stop being treated. He wanted to stop taking his medication immediately. In his words, as you have probably already seen in the footage, he wanted the good lord to take him away naturally, whenever his time came. He also wanted to be able to spend his last days on earth with a clear mind, and a clear view of the Brighton sea."

"Was this before or after Andrew and Mr Dupont came in?"

"Before."

"Were any of you against it?"

"All of us, yes. We did not think it to be prudent, and neither did his doctor, as we all knew he was effectively signing his death sentence. But he would not accept any arguments contrary to his position. He said he would refuse to take his medication, he wanted to spend the small time he had left in his life as a person, not a vegetable. We had no choice but to accept his decision. He repeated every single day after that, around six AM and six PM, that it was his wish not to take his medication anymore, and that nobody should be blamed for his certain death. He also made me film it every time. I didn't feel it was necessary to hand all the clips to the police, but they are at your disposal, should you like to have them."

"No, I don't think it's necessary. Thank you though. Did he inform anyone else that he had stopped taking his medication?"

"No. He told us not to tell anyone about it, nor to release the video until after his death. Not even Andrew was to be informed. He also asked me and nurse Piotrowka to keep telling people that his mind was not working properly, as if he would still be taking his medication. Which, in a way, it was not entirely false. We did not know for sure how long it would take for him to recover his faculties completely after he stopped taking it. There is a big discussion within the medical community about it."

"Did he tell you why he made that decision?"

"Not beside the reasons he gave before."

With that, it looked like Steve's questions had come to an end. He asked if any of us had anything to ask, and I was surprised to have been included in that question. I was also surprised that Hildegard did not have any questions. Felicity then printed the statement, nurse Muller read it, signed and handed it back to her. He asked one more question before leaving.

"Should I instruct nurse Piotrowka to come give a statement as well? They said they are available to come, but I personally think they would probably not have any further information, as their shift is usually the quiet one. Not much happens overnight."

"No, I don't think it is necessary for them to come. Thank them on my behalf, for offering."

Nurse Muller said goodbye and left. I opened my mouth to discuss what we just heard, but both Hildegard and Steve apologised and said they had to leave to take care of something. Steve left, Hildegard stayed behind and handed me a piece of paper.

"You might find this very interesting: the previous will from Lord Honeywell, the one that is now invalidated. It had been made in August last year, when he found out about the cancer. I think you will enjoy this."

She then said I could go home whenever I felt like it, because neither of them would not be back that day. In fact, I would probably only see them again at the memorial, the next day. Hildegard told me we could meet in town and take the bus together, so we made a plan to meet at the clock tower at a quarter past ten. After she left, I started reading the old will.

It was all very standard: It basically stated that in the event of Lord Honeywell's death, an amount of money was to be set aside to cover the immediate costs, like cremation and funeral, plus enough to maintain his properties for a year, and finally the equivalent of one year's salary to be paid to each of his private employees - not including the ones working for the law firm.

His property in London would go to Andrew, whilst his house in Hove and the apartment where Jack lived in the Marina would go to Jack. The flat where Andrew lived, which I believe was rented, was not listed in the will. Ten percent of his fortune would go to the charity Jack was working for. The rest of his assets would be divided between Jack and Andrew, with fifty percent going to Jack and forty going to Andrew, but he did not specify what would go to whom.

Dupont would get full ownership of the business, but Lord Honeywell was very clear that he did not want it to continue with his name. And that was it, apart from some other technicalities.

I finished reading it and went home. I used my afternoon and evening free to do some laundry and catch up on some TV shows, but I could not really focus on anything and ended up going to bed early. I could not sleep, my brain would not turn itself off. What was I missing? What was I not seeing? What did Hildegard see that I didn't, when we visited the victim's father? I was also starting to feel a bit impatient with the situation. Why had nobody been arrested yet? What was taking so long? It felt like the case was getting colder, the press did not care about it that much anymore. There was a small note about it on some papers, a small segment on the news on TV, but the country had moved on. Did our murderer also move on already? Hildegard guaranteed me that someone would be arrested soon, but I started questioning her conviction.

I was quiet on the bus journey to the Honeywell's house the next morning. Hildegard noticed it, and tried to cheer me up.

"Don't let it get you down, mate. We are almost there."

"I don't see anything happening. We are getting colder, we are starting to forget about it. The country is moving on."

"Which is exactly what we wanted. We want our murderer to think that we are off their scent. We want to let them think that they've won, they've beaten us. They got away with the perfect crime. We want them to relax and feel confident, feel like nobody can catch them. So they become careless. It is happening already."

But I felt very blase about it, and I didn't talk anymore until we arrived at the house. There were some twenty people in the living room, amongst them all the people we met so far: Miss Ahmet, Mr Dupont, Miss Ling, Mr and Mrs Smith, the two nurses, Ms Dolores and Mr Andrew. Steve was not anywhere to be seen. I was once again curious as to why Alisson Ling was there - as far as I was aware, she had left the country and was on a holiday in Greece. She told us that Andrew contacted her, wanting to talk to her about something, and she decided to come. She could see no harm in coming back to England. She said they would have a meeting after the memorial. Andrew denied it categorically.

"Why would I contact that ghastly woman? I was hoping I would never have to see her again. I mean, I suppose I had to agree to her being here, she found Jack, but to tell people I want to talk to her? About what? That's a bit much."

The memorial was nice and simple. Nobody made a speech, people just talked to each other. The food was exceptional, and the drinks were of good quality. Hildegard was close to me, and we started to talk about something trivial, but I was interrupted by a phone call from a number I did not recognise.

"You have to take that, mate?"

"No, not really, I don't know this number. Let me silence it."

But the number called again, and again, and on the fourth time, I got worried that it could have been something important, so I went into the library, at the other side of the marble staircase, and closed the door behind me to draw the noise away. The person on the other side talked very fast. There was a faint sound of a siren coming from the street outside that grew louder and louder, and I couldn't understand what the caller was saying. The siren then stopped, and I asked the caller once again.

"Sorry, I couldn't understand you before. Can you repeat what you said?"

"This is Nisha! I have a package here from your mum, I am standing in front of your flat. 27 Preston Road?"

"Sorry, I think you have the wrong number."

The person apologised and hung up. I put my phone back into my pocket, opened the door of the library and I saw a big commotion. People were all standing up, whispering loudly, gasping and a circle had formed, surrounding something I could not see. I seem to have missed most of the drama, I could only catch the ending of a sentence: 'you are under arrest for the murder of Jack Honeywell!'

The circle opened slowly and the people inside it started walking towards the door. Someone was handcuffed, and was being taken away by a police officer I did not recognise. But I *did* recognise the person being arrested...

The ripped pieces of fabric

It was Alisson Ling. I had been right all along to suspect her. I could not stop myself from bragging to Hildegard, very excitedly:

"Ling! It all makes sense! The threatening, the paper interview, the disappearance to Greece and the overconfidence to come back here. I knew it!"

"Hmm, not so fast. You should look closer. Wait for it..."

Right behind Alisson came Steve, taking Andrew Honeywell by his side, also handcuffed. I am pretty sure my jaw dropped. Andrew? Arrested? With Alisson? No, that did not make any sense. Hildegard gently closed my mouth, which was wide open. I tried to ask what was happening, but I could barely articulate a sentence.

"Wha... No! It can't. But... Wait, I don't get it. They hated each other! Was that all a lie?"

"I will explain it all in a minute. Please gather the other four and the staff in the library, I will have a quick chat with detective Pritchard and meet you all there."

The majority of people present walked towards the outside of the house following the police officers, making it difficult for me to gather the people I was looking for. Finally, I managed to get everyone into the library: Lily Ahmet, Anna and Martin Smith, Cedric Dupont, and nurses Muller and Piotrowka. They all looked equally stunned by this recent development, except maybe nurse Muller, who looked more relaxed. Soon Hildegard came into the room with Steve, and they closed the door behind them. Dolores was the last one to come in, after making sure all the other guests had left. Steve started talking.

"I won't be able to stay for long, but I wanted to be the one to tell you about Alisson Ling. I will leave the tale of Andrew Honeywell for Mrs Hildegard to tell you all, it's only fair. He was her client - and it was her theory, after all."

It would have been possible to hear an eyelash fall on the floor; We all stood there in absolute silence waiting to hear the story. Steve went on.

"Miss Ling is what we started calling a happy accident in this case. When she came into this investigation, we thought she was a mere witness to an incident. Back then, we didn't even know if there was any foul play involved in the death of Jack. I guess she was very unlucky to have had the spotlight shone over her like that."

He took a breath and continued.

"The first thing that called my attention to her was actually a statement from Andrew: he said something about how Jack was threatening to denounce her to the marina management, and how she was lucky he wouldn't escalate this further. What would be further than the management? It could only have gone two possible ways: the city council or the police. That prompted me to start asking around if there was any investigation involving something in the marina, and it turns out my hunch was right: there was an ongoing investigation in the marina."

He paused again, and I wouldn't be surprised if he was doing it on purpose, for a dramatic effect.

"The police had been investigating a network of contraband and smuggling in Brighton, and there was some intelligence pointing to someone operating in the marina. And then, a few days later, an article came out in the paper mentioning, once again, smuggling and contraband, but this time involving Jack. It could not have been just a coincidence. We initially thought they were working together, and she might have murdered him due to some issue between them two. But that theory did not pan out. So we asked ourselves: could Alisson Ling have killed Jack?"

It sounded obvious to me.

"Yes, to prevent him from going to the police?"

"Sure, this was the obvious idea. But as I said, it didn't fit with the murder we had. First of all, why would she want to bring the attraction of the police to her next door flat, when she was involved with something illegal herself? Also, why would she leave the door open? She could have left him there to he discovered a long time later. Why would she be the one to come in and 'accidentally' find him, then call the police? Finally, it sounded a bit far-fetched that they would have a friendly drink together - even though methanol would have been easy for her to come across, seeing as she was involved in selling spiked drinks."

He made another dramatic pause, a short one this time.

"No, Alisson Ling was not the murderer we were looking for. She could not have been, it didn't fit. It didn't make sense. Besides, we would later come to learn that she also had a solid alibi that prevented her from committing this crime."

"Didn't her friend betray her and say she left them?"

I interrupted Steve without thinking about it, and I braced myself for his reaction. To my surprise, he just smiled and continued.

"Patience, kid, there is more to be explained, but I don't want to get ahead of myself. Oh, and her holiday in Greece? It was not really a holiday, she was there on business, to bring more illegal stuff into this country. The Gatwick team was ready to arrest her as soon as she landed, but we asked them to delay the arrest, with the promise we would keep an eye on her: if she sneezed we would be there with a tissue. We wanted to dismantle the whole operation, and we did it earlier today. Miss Ling was the last person arrested from the whole network. Arresting her *here* was my personal touch, to add a bit of flourish to everything."

He stopped, smiled at Hildegard, and said a few more words.

"I will now let Mrs Hildegard dazzle you like she did me, when she presented me her theory. Unfortunately I cannot be here to see it happening, I need to go back to the police station to start the paperwork. I just ask you all to have faith."

He looked directly at me when he said that, and I understood the message. He said his goodbyes and Hildegard took over. She started speaking eloquently, knowing exactly where to pause and which words to emphasise to create an effect. She knew how to command a room.

"I would like to tell you all the story of a young kid called Andrew Honeywell. He was only two years old when he lost both his parents. I won't go into the full psychology of it, because I am not qualified to do so, but you can imagine the effect this would have on a child. Maybe not directly, on the surface, as the child cannot really understand the world around them yet. But if we look deeper, things happened in his mind and in his heart that would be part of his personality for the rest of his life. Parents are our first point of reference in the world."

We were all listening very attentively. She continued her speech.

"He was taken in by his uncle and aunt, but it has never been the same for him. He was never treated the same way as his cousin Jack Honeywell, the official child of Sarah and James Honeywell. Especially by his uncle - who told me so himself. That created a sense of inferiority in him, that he was never as good as his cousin, and he would never be. He was constantly being denied that, and there was nothing he could do to change it, because it was out of his control. He grew up in a world unfair to him. And it didn't get better with time. Even we referred to his uncle as uncle, despite Andrew calling him 'dad'. Miss Ahmet here used the words 'he was only the nephew, there's no pizazz'. He would forever be the nephew, the next best thing, as long as Jack would exist. He was doomed to live in Jack's shadow."

Lily looked defiant and said, defensively, that she didn't lie.

"You are correct Miss Ahmet, but the truth can also hurt. Especially from you, when it came to Andrew. I would not be surprised if you said that exact phrase to him directly, seeing how you are usually unaware of anyone other than yourself. I don't know if you ever suspected, for example, that Andrew was in love with you since the first time he met you. Not that it would have mattered to you anyway."

Lily was laughing and making bitchy comments under her breath. Hildegard addressed her very angrily.

"You might think this is all funny, the same way you think life and other people's feelings are a joke. Your ex boyfriend died, and when you came in all you could think about was how this affected you, your life, your 'brand' and your followers. You later gave Andrew a chance, but not because you were interested in him. You gave him a chance because he was your easiest option, the next best thing. He was there already. He would now have money and fame, all the things you wanted. You are an embarrassment to women, people like you help fuel age old sexists and misogynist behaviours."

"Whatevs, babe. There's a sheikh in Dubai who wants to take me out. I didn't know how to get out of this thing with Andrew, but now that he's been arrested, I assume we're done. Thanks for arresting him, you just saved my life!"

"Please, just leave."

"Yeah, I'm bored of you, girl. Oof, you can talk! And your makeup, hun! I'll send you a link to some tutorials, basic beginner stuff. You can totally look better than that."

Her phone started ringing.

"That's Brenner. My efficient gay boy. He should be here. Ciao, Amore! Yes, I am about to walk out the door as a free woman for the sheikh."

She left the room. Mr Dupont spoke next, his voice had a note of disgust.

"What a horrible selfish woman. I told Andrew to stay away from her!"

Hildegard looked at him with a curious gaze.

"You are the one to talk, Mr Dupont. I believe you went to Andrew and told him you wanted to keep the business going, and how you would do anything for it to happen. Your intentions were to intimidate him, giving the impression you had something to do with Jack's death. That did not work with Andrew, for obvious reasons. But he knew how incompetent you were, and how you would destroy the business in no time. It was part of his plan - but we will get to that. Your ego did not let you see it. Worse, you went to Lord Honeywell and told him what you and Andrew decided, and that his will could not change it, because Andrew would also have rights over the name Honeywell. Lord Honeywell might have shared with you his suspicions about Andrew - oh yes, he knew Andrew was the killer, he was the one who pointed me in this direction. But you decided to side with Andrew anyway, the man who presumably killed your partner's son, showing your true allegiance and priorities. Against the man who made you who you are. You also downplayed the suspicions he had about Andrew, showing that you were really ready to do anything to get what you wanted. Although I am sure Andrew would never use you. He knew you were not competent enough to defend him. You are like Miss Ahmet: you disgust me, just like she did."

"I don't have to stay here and be insulted like this. I hope you are prepared to back up that defamation, you can surely expect a lawsuit."

"In that case, I sincerely hope you'll be the one to persecute me personally - I'll sleep soundly at night knowing I have nothing to worry about."

Mr Dupont got up and left, slamming the door behind him. Hildegard pulled herself together and continued.

"Now where was I? The situation with Miss Ahmer is just one example of how Andrew resented Jack: he wanted to reclaim his place in the world, a place he thought belonged to him but was unfairly handed to Jack instead. He also truly believed that Jack was having an affair with a married woman - not only Jack stole the girl Andrew was in love with, he was now stealing someone else's girl: Anna Smith."

Anna Smith interrupted her.

"Jack and I were only friends."

"Oh yes, Mrs Smith, you are correct. At least in part of what you said. Jack was *your* friend, but you were never *his*. You suspected something about him, I don't know how, probably by working with close proximity to the family. And you saw an opportunity to exploit it in your favour when he confirmed your suspicions: Jack Honeywell was gay. Only his father, Dolores and the nurses knew, he hadn't even told Andrew. But somehow you made him comfortable enough to come out to you, and he also confided in you that his father did not accept his sexuality. You pretended to be his friend, but always trying to take advantage. You and your husband, you both wanted to make an extra buck."

"How dare you?"

"I imagine you told Jack that things were difficult at home, because your close friendship was bringing you issues with your husband, and you didn't want to betray him and tell your husband about his sexuality. But you had already betrayed him. Your husband was never jealous of you, because he knew everything from day one. I don't know which one of you came up with the plan, probably you, I cannot see your husband thinking of something so clever on his own. You both managed to score an all expenses paid trip to the Maldives 'to save your marriage'. It was the least Jack could do for you, after all the 'support' you offered him. I also believe Jack told you about his issues with Miss Ling - that's the only explanation to how you mentioned it in that dreadful article."

"Which article? The one in the tabloid? You can't be serious! I have nothing to do with that article!"

"Why, yes, that tabloid story, it was you. It had your scent all over it. Pretending to be a neighbour, how genius was that? There was actually a neighbour involved, nobody would ever suspect you. But you were greedy, the holiday and the considerable sum you probably got from the paper for the story was not enough. You went to the source, to the man who could give you much more: Lord Honeywell. You told him about leaking it all to the press, blackmailed him to keep your mouth. But you had already made the deal with the paper, they had already paid you, you just made sure to get even more from someone else before it was published. Lord Honeywell said he could not believe you went through with it and called you an 'evil bitch'. The women he hired and had by his side all these years. You betrayed a dead man who believed you were his friend, you sold your soul to a cheap tabloid and you blackmailed a dying man who gave you a job. I cannot imagine how much lower someone can go. You two are disgusting human beings, just like the other two."

Martin got up and started speaking, his tone and manners were very intimidating.

"I won't admit anyone talking to me missus like that."

"This tone will not fly with me, mate. I know your type very well. Open your mouth again, and I will destroy your life. Try me, if you don't believe me. It would be better for you two if you get up and leave, and never come back into this house again. If you ever come close to these people, I will make it my personal mission to ruin your life. Scum like you don't have a place in this world. You make me want to vomit."

I have never imagined hearing Hildegard say such strong words about anyone. I was really taken aback by the way she spoke, even though she had all the reasons to do so. It seemed to have worked, though - they left, but not before calling her names I won't repeat. I was in a state of shock with how they all reacted, and everything that had been said about them. The words from Lord Honeywell echoed in my head once again: 'they are all lions'. But I still had many questions, and Hildegard seemed to be able to see the curiosity in my face.

"Alright, it's only us five now. We expurgated the worms. I can tell you everything. It won't be easy for most of you, but it's the truth. We talked about how Andrew felt inferior to Jack, due to the way he was treated his whole life. But there was a dynamic, a homeostasis, an equilibrium that kept things in balance for Andrew: Lady Sarah. She would provide him with love and attention, she would keep him away from the edge. But, as we all know, Lady Sarah passed away, and that tipped the scale to one side."

The mention of the name of Lady Sarah sent a ripple effect through the room. Everyone looked extremely sad. I had the feeling that she was really admired by everyone there, even the ones who never met her. Hildegard continued, her tone became more calm and compassionate.

"But there was one more thing that helped push Andrew over the edge. Something I did not want to discuss in front of the others. Now, I will start going into conjecture here, although I am pretty sure I am correct in my assumptions. After discovering the cancer and the realisation he would certainly die, Lord Honeywell started thinking about his legacy and how he could make amends before he would be gone. It's a common feeling amongst people with terminal conditions."

It made sense: we have all seen it happening many times. Hildegard went on.

"I am fairly certain Lord Honeywell had something to do with the death of his brother and sister in law, Andrew's parents. He hinted it to me, in between lines, when we met. I also have reasons to suspect that Lord Honeywell was Andrew's biological father, making Jack and Andrew half brothers, not cousins."

That last revelation hit me like a slap on the face. No wonder they looked so much like each other! Hildegard looked at Nurse Muller and talked to him.

"And it was you, nurse Muller, who told me that it is likely his patient disclosed all this to Andrew, thinking he was talking to Jack, because of the way the medicine altered his perception of the world. I don't know why he would want to confess it to Jack, but I can speculate: he probably wanted Jack to take care of Andrew after he died. Jack was older, and his father probably wanted to pass over to him the responsibility he had taken years ago. I can only imagine Andrew's feelings when he heard that. He finally saw that the man who destroyed his life was also the one who neglected him and treated him as second to Jack this whole time, despite being his biological father."

I remembered the meeting we had in that house and things started to fall into place. It all made perfect sense. But Hildegard was not even close to finishing.

"Life had once again been unfair to him: his aunt, the one with whom he was most connected, was now dead, and he was left with the killer of his parents. He knew that Lord Honeywell was going to die due to his condition, but it probably would be a while until it actually happened. Andrew himself told us that his uncle was receiving the best treatment money could buy. So it all started to come together for him. He wanted to reclaim his place, to get back the life that, in his point of view, was so unfairly taken away from him. He also wanted to get revenge on his uncle. It all pointed to one direction: Jack had to die.

I was feeling extremely uncomfortable with this. It all made perfect sense, and all I could do was judge Andrew for saying the wrong stuff whenever we met. I never looked deep inside his feelings. But I tried not to get lost within my thoughts, so I could keep up with Hildegard's explanation.

“This would achieve the best outcome for Andrew: his uncle was dying, and without Jack, he would be the only Honeywell left. He would inherit all the money, properties, titles, the women, everything that he felt he had been neglected... In his head, this would make him a real Honeywell, nobody else could ever take this away from him again. It would also have a side effect: to inflict a tremendous amount of pain on his uncle, the man he held responsible for everything bad that happened to him. No parent should live to see their children die - I don't have kids, but I imagine this is the worst possible pain a person can feel.”

Hildegard stopped. Even for her, this was a difficult subject. She had a bit of water, took a deep breath, and continued her explanation.

“He started looking for ways to kill Jack and escape from being blamed for it. And then there was the Christmas party, all his potential suspects fell right on his lap. His uncle's partner, unethical and unscrupulous, unhappy with the end of their life's work - here once again Andrew saw his uncle destroying someone else's life. The girlfriend, who only thought about herself, the one who rejected him before, appalled that Jack wanted to end the relationship. But it was not enough that Jack had stolen the girl he liked, he was now doing the same with another man, stealing his wife. Remember, Andrew did not know Jack was gay, or that there was a plan from both Mr and Mrs Smith. He found his suspects and became more and more sure his plan could be done."

I thought about the picture, but did not want to mention anything and interrupt Holdegard, who kept explaining.

"Andrew started planning the crime after the Christmas party. I believe the method came to him in a conversation with Jack about Ling - another potential suspect that conveniently came up in conversation. Jack probably mentioned something about spiked drinks, and Andrew thought about the plan of spiking his drink with methanol. He told us himself, Jack did not drink much. Would have been an easy thing to do, to have a drink together, celebrate the new year. We found a search history in Andrew's browser related to methanol poisoning, accessed on the evening of December twenty-ninth - the day he got back home after staying with Jack. Why did he stay with Jack? To learn things that could help his plan succeed. He now had to find the best opportunity to do it, and that opportunity presented itself in a news article about me."

I suddenly remembered.

"The medal!"

"Exactly. He read the article, saw my name and the logistics of the crime formed in his head. It was so simple, yet so clever. I don't believe Jack had ever told him his life was in danger. Andrew just said it to justify why Jack would come to my office. It was crucial for the plan that Jack went to my office."

The others were still there, listening, but the conversation became dominated by us two, talking to each other. I spoke next.

"But how could Jack go to your office if he was not afraid for his life?"

"He did not. Jack Honeywell was never at my office."

"We saw the footage."

"Yes, we saw *a* footage, where someone who looked like Jack, dressed in many clothes, a sports cap and sunglasses, visited my office. But I can tell you with a hundred percent assurance that was not Jack, that was Andrew. Pretending to be Jack. Don't you see? He did it to manipulate time. It was a very clever plan: Andrew came home from work, allegedly feeling sick, talked to his neighbour to establish his alibi, but instead of staying in like he said, he travelled to Brighton, went straight to the Marina, made sure Ling was not home and poisoned Jack. He then walked to my office pretending to be Jack, stayed there long enough to create a second alibi, left the building and travelled back home, in time to see his neighbour again later in the evening, solidifying his first alibi."

"That is incredible."

"And yet, entirely true. If Jack was alive and well between four-thirty and five, Andrew could not have killed him, in case he would have been seen anywhere in Brighton earlier. And he was seen. Remember when Dupont said he saw Andrew in the lanes, and we thought he confused them both? He really *did* see Andrew. He knew those boys since they were kids, he saw them growing up right in front of his eyes. He would never confuse them."

"That makes perfect sense!"

"And Andrew knew that he would have been caught in the CCTV of the train station, so once again, if Jack was alive at the time he was in my office, Andrew could not have been blamed for it, the time would not match. When 'Jack' would get home in the Marina after the office visit, Andrew would already be halfway home on the train, so he couldn't do it."

"He really thought this through!"

"After 'Jack' came into the office, I wondered: if he was so worried about his life, why wouldn't he write down his details and have me call him right away? The answer was very simple: besides not being worried about his life, Jack was left handed, and Andrew was right handed. Remember when he signed his statement and the pen broke, how he flexed his stained right arm? Writing down his details would have given that away. Andrew said it himself: that was their tell growing up. But Andrew did make two mistakes that day, whilst in my office. First, he hit his right fist down the table, and second, he took off his sunglasses. We have seen detective Pritchard hit his left fist down the table multiple times, and he is left handed. Usually one does involuntary movements with one's dominant arm. As for the sunglasses, Miss Hughes could not tell those were Andrew's eyes, because she didn't know either of them. But I prepared a small test to check my suspicions, and I was dead on the money."

"Felicity's grandson's photoshop skills!"

"Exactly! I created several pictures, some of Jack with Andrew's eyes, some of Andrew with Jack's eyes, some of them just the way they were, and some of their eyes mixed with random people I found in photo libraries online. I asked Miss Hughes just to identify the eyes she saw that day, not the face. And what did you think happened? She identified Andrew's eyes correctly every single time, regardless of the face they were on. Never Jack's. I made sure to do it as part of a statement and with the involvement of detective Pritchard and Dr Sanjay, to make it legal and admissible in court later. That test showed me I was right, so I started looking in the right places."

"His flat?"

"That too, but it's much simpler than that. Dr Sanjay said that he didn't ask for the CCTV footage from the train station because there were no trains to the Marina, so we did not have any reason to look for train station footage. If someone commits a murder in London, would you look for clues in New York? We were looking at the wrong places. But once we knew where to look, we requested the train station's footage from earlier that day and from right after he left my office, and there he was, clear as day. Dressed the same way. There was also footage of him in the train station of his town in Essex, further corroborating my theory. We also found footage of him walking to the Marina earlier that afternoon. It also added up that it didn't look like

Jack had left the house on such a cold day based on what was in his wardrobe and washing machine - I think you remember me checking it. The more we looked in the right places, the more proof we found."

I was overwhelmed. It all sounded fantastic, but completely plausible. Hildegard didn't show signs of stopping.

"One more thing that caught my attention was how the board in Jack's office only had family pictures, but also the one picture of four strangers at a party. I believe that picture was planted by Andrew, to indicate all the possible suspects and exonerate him. Remember the question I asked you when we left Lord Honeywell's house? 'What is the first thing we know about this case? When is the first thing *we* know about Jack Honeywell?' If you think about it, it all came from Andrew. *He* told me it was Jack who came to my office. *He* told me Jack was fearing for his life. *He* even alerted me that Jack was the victim. He needed me to be in the investigation for his plan to work. You'll probably remember his words when I asked him if he wanted the truth to come out: 'I want you to be part of this investigation'. In fact, I helped Andrew obstruct it."

"You did *what*?"

"Not intentionally, of course. But it was me, I was responsible for the wrong time of death! I was the one who brought the information of 'Jack' having been in my office into the investigation, and that was used as the base to estimate the time of death, differing from what the doctor had previously thought. If you think back, you'll remember the doctor said he first thought Jack had been dead for more than twelve hours when he first examined the body. Dr Sanjay was right all along, and if it wasn't for me, he would have established the time of death much earlier."

"One small detail, and that was enough to send the investigation in a completely different direction. This case did not cease to fascinate me."

"*Andrew* was also the one who told us to investigate Ling and the Smiths. He was conveniently vague about Ahmet and

Dupont, because he was not very interested in either of them being associated with the murder. With the new estimate of the time of death, all of the other suspects were now eliminated, as they all had alibis. It was the ultimate validation that my theory was right. Although I still think there is one more thing to come, the thing that will be the last proof that Andrew is the murderer: the letter from Lord Honeywell."

"The one he requested to keep sealed until after we found the killer?"

"Yes. Remember when I said earlier that Lord Honeywell knew it was Andrew who killed Jack? I have a strong suspicion that Andrew confessed the murder to his uncle."

"Why would he do that?"

"It is the ultimate redemption strike - I can almost hear the words he might have used: 'you killed my parents, I then killed the thing you loved the most. Now you will only see him again when you are dead. Maybe, if you are lucky enough, he will come to pick you up'. And I have reasons to believe this was done on the third of January, when he came to stay over after the body was discovered. Lord Honeywell was still under medication, it wasn't until later he stopped taking it. Think about it, the two looked like each other. In normal circumstances the father would have been able to tell them apart, but his mind was not in its regular state and he just received shocking news that Jack was dead. He might have thought it was Jack he was talking to, hence why he mentioned that Jack killed himself. Riddled with guilt for not accepting his son's sexuality, he immediately assumed this as a possibility. Later, when he could think clearer, he probably realised what actually happened - and shared his suspicions with Mr Dupont. He also pointed me in this direction, but he would never flat out tell me."

"I just can't grasp the idea of Andrew being so... evil!"

"At the end of the day, it is not for any of us to judge this. In the grand scheme of things, it would have been better for anyone other than Andrew to be accused of murder, but I would like to believe that he did not want anyone else to be accused. He envisioned a plan for a crime that would remain unsolved.

Which is probably why he threw in so many suspects, built so many alibis…"

"That does not make any sense."

"Doesn't it? Jack is dead, and he managed to hurt his uncle. I don't think he wanted anyone else to suffer, regardless of how awful all those people all are. I would not be so quick to declare Andrew an evil person. There's many nuances there, many things to be discussed. But that is me, maybe I have a kind way of seeing the world. We cannot know for sure unless he is ever willing to talk about it."

She seemed to have concluded her explanation. We were all stunned, and our faces showed it. Dolores was crying. One by one, we left the room. I needed a break, I needed to go away, I needed to digest it all. I excused myself, left the room and walked out of that house. My feet were moving, but I had no clue where they were taking me. I did not know where to go.

Chapter Twelve

This is just the beginning

The train was crossing a beautiful valley, moving slowly over the tracks of the viaduct. Everything was covered in snow all around, in all directions, and the late afternoon sun shone a dark hue of yellow, making the landscape look like a painting. It was Friday, the third of February, and I was on my way back to Brighton from London.

It's been exactly three weeks since Alisson Ling and Andrew Honeywell had been arrested; Three weeks since I last saw all those people that, for two weeks, became a big part of my life. Where were they now, what were they doing, how were they getting on with their lives?

I did have some pieces of information. After the arrests, Mr Dupont announced to the media he was closing Honeywell-Dupont with immediate effect. I don't know what drove his decision, but I could assume that, without the support of Andrew, he was left with no option. It was quite the embarrassment, seeing that he gave an interview some days before affirming he would continue with the firm. His team would start transferring their ongoing cases to other law practices - Anna Smith was responsible for overseeing that process. Mr Dupont also announced that he was leaving the UK for the time being and returning to his homeland Belgium, blaming Brexit for his decision. I had a feeling that Mrs Smith would eventually join him there.

The Smiths managed to avoid the spotlight since the conclusion of the cases. Many papers attributed statements to both Anna and Martin, but the pair denied everything categorically. They both seemed to have escaped from the whole drama unharmed - even when their name was cited in the papers, they would give short and concise statements denying everything with not many more details to follow. Those statements always came from Anna. There were some reports of Martin getting drunk in a pub and saying he knew things that could turn the case upside down, but that was also quickly denied by his wife afterwards.

On the other hand, Lily Ahmet enjoyed the spotlight as much as she could. She used her position in the case to increase her social media presence, but also to expand it into traditional media, like TV shows. She would appear in morning shows, give interviews, write articles for papers, and had recently announced that she would join the cast of a reality show for singles looking for love, filmed in Dubai. She also announced plans to release a book detailing her relationship with the Honeywells, but it was met with a lukewarm reception, despite the promise of incendiary details. She did manage to exceed the mark of a million followers, which I guess was a big achievement for her.

Alisson Ling was completely ignored by the press altogether, especially the sensationalist tabloids. There was a small note on a serious paper about her arrest the following day, and it was reported locally by TV stations, but it never even made it to national news. I had no clue what had happened to her afterwards.

The big sensation had been the arrest of Andrew and his involvement with the murder. The newspapers could not get enough of it, digging old pictures, talking to old acquaintances, telling every story from his past they could find. And also coming up with all kinds of speculations and theories about him.

Some said he was pure evil, others made assumptions about the state of his mental health, whilst others went straight to conspiracy theories, like one that debated he was a spy from a foreign country trying to destroy the British Empire. Andrew himself remained silent. He pleaded guilty, but his lawyers insisted on him being charged with manslaughter instead of murder. The judge initially denied the motion, but once the letter from Lord Honeywell was made public, the lawyers submitted a petition to request another analysis of the motion.

The new will from Lord Honeywell was similar to his previous one: cover the costs of his funeral, properties, private staff and ten percent to charity. Everything else was left to Andrew, and Andrew alone. The letter was also published. It was a big surprise for everyone that was not present in the room that day, including the three other suspects. But it was nothing me and the staff hadn't heard before - as it contained basically everything Hildegard said it would, with more details. He assumed full responsibility for the murder of his brother and sister-in-law and indirect responsibility for everything that led to Andrew murdering Jack. He also requested Andrew to have the best defence available in the country, whatever it would cost.

I felt sadness every time I thought about Andrew. He was a lovely young man when I met him, and I never expected him to be able to murder someone. I could appreciate the fact that he killed someone, and that was something horrendous, but I felt a sort of compassion for him. Hildegard, who was sitting across from me in the train, could read it in my face.

"You're thinking about Andrew again, aren't you?"

"It shocks me how well you know me already. And yes, I am wondering what will happen to him now, if he will be convicted, if he will spend his life in jail."

"I would expect you to be thinking about him. This is the goal - from his late uncle and from his team of lawyers. They want everyone in the country to feel connected to Andrew, sorry for him, feel like he's their younger brother, their younger son. That he is actually a good guy, who was put in this position by adversities in life. This is crucial for the defence team - and remember, his uncle was a great defence attorney, he knew exactly how that can make or break a trial. The view of society can always influence the way someone will be judged."

"Wow, this is very manipulative. And it works!"

"This is how lawyers operate. They need to convince a jury that someone is either guilty or not. They will use all techniques available. I am sure the prosecution has some tricks up its sleeves as well. But none of this is our business anymore. Over the years you should learn to detach yourself from the cases. Our part is over now. We have built a solid case for the prosecution, but the defence also has a lot to lean on. It will be interesting to see what comes out of it. But I won't lose sleep over the outcome - it is not in our hands anymore. Although we might be called to testify at some point."

"I think I would like to follow it, see how it turns out. We always think it's over when the person is arrested, but I guess it is just the beginning."

"You are right, arresting someone is just the first part. There is much more to come. But while you are there, thinking about Andrew, I have my empathy somewhere else. I can't help but think about what will happen to Alisson Ling."

"Ling? She was caught doing something deplorable, and she has to pay for her actions."

"And Andrew doesn't? Do you think smuggling and contrabanding is worse than taking the life of someone else?"

"Mrs Hildegard, I am not judging the actions, but the circumstances surrounding them."

"Oh, I think it's time you start calling me Helga. And yes, the circumstances, here is where the bias lives. Andrew is male, straight and white. Right off the bat, he is in a much better position than Ling. Now throw in the fact that he comes from a rich and well connected family of lawyers who are able to provide him with the best defence one can get in this country. And what does Ling have? She is a woman of colour who will probably end up with a public defender - don't get me wrong, there are great public defenders in this country - but statistically speaking, her chances are much smaller than Andrew's, in the grand scheme of things. I won't go into the merits of which crime is worse, but I can't help but think about her fate. More than Andrew's."

I felt very embarrassed. Hildegard was right, I was one more person following that pattern cleverly devised by Andrew's defending team. She noticed it upset me, and was quick to change the subject.

"It was nice to see Steve Pritchard yesterday."

The sudden mention of Steve made me grin. I hadn't thought about him in a long time. After the case was concluded, Hildegard had been very fair with her position: she insisted that she was only a consulting part, and Steve was the lead investigator of the case. Many people speculated that she was the one who solved it, but Steve got most of the credit, and she did not dispute that fact.

Consequently, he was offered the position of Head of PR for the Sussex Police. Hildegard was adamant that he should accept it, making the argument that his ability to charm people would be very useful in that position. There would also be a substantial pay rise. He did seem frustrated with his abilities as a detective and there seemed to be no downsides to this job offer. Therefore he accepted it.

He started working as head of PR the week following the arrests, but the official swearing in ceremony had been on the second of February, the day before our trip to London, and Steve looked like a completely different person. Three weeks felt like three months for him. He was well groomed, well dressed, but the biggest difference was his mood: he looked happy, he found his right place in the police.

His previous post as lead investigator was still vacant, and there was a rumour someone was coming from the MET Police. I wondered what the new person's opinion of Hildegard would be - it would be infinitely easier for future cases to have a lead investigator on our side. I smiled with that thought. A month ago, I was taking this same journey, seeing the first sights of Brighton from the train, dreading to come live in this place. Now I was entering Brighton again, thinking about possible future cases.

I also realised that I was starting to feel hungry. Luckily for me, I had been invited to have dinner at Hildegard's that night. I would finally try Jill's famous spag bol. I had met Jill already, on a couple of occasions, and I was delighted by her. She was even more outgoing and extroverted than Hildegard. Both of them were very welcoming to me and we were slowly becoming good friends. But, most importantly, they took me in. I gained two lovely chosen mothers.

We took the bus number seven in the direction of the Marina, but this time we stopped halfway, in Kemptown. The bus ride was quick, and very shortly we were entering the flat. They lived in a lovely, large flat right on the seafront, located on the first floor, which meant a partial sea view. But they had a massive garden, one that is almost impossible to find in Kemptown flats. I couldn't wait for the summer, in the hopes I would be invited to enjoy that garden and all its potential.

We sat down at the table, Jill brought in the tray right out of the oven. It was bubbling and the cheese crust was baked to perfection. She had also prepared some garlic bread that added a lovely and inviting perfume to the room. I was starving, and that explosion of sensory *stimuli* did not help. I started to get terrified that my stomach would roar and embarrass me. I wanted this dinner to be the first of many.

We started serving ourselves and I couldn't wait to dig in. The first bite was enough to confirm this was the best spaghetti bolognese I've ever had and I practically devoured it. Hildegard was laughing.

"I *would* judge you if this would be any other dish. But I know how good this is, especially the first time you try it. I think that's when I realised I wanted to spend the rest of my life with this woman, when I ate her bolognese. But there's one more thing..."

"Is there more food?"

"Why yes, we have dessert, but that's not what I mean. This sauce is vegetarian."

"No way!"

"Jill and I have been vegetarian for years."

Jill took over the explanation.

"It's all in the way you add layers of flavours. Yeast extract and treacle are great to give it a meaty taste. You'd be surprised with everything you can create by mixing some unusual ingredients."

Indeed I was surprised. I had a sip of the beautiful *Carmenere* they opened, put another fork into my mouth and suddenly remembered the first time I had a full conversation with Hildegard. It had only been a month, but it felt like years had passed.

"This brings me back to that Italian cafe in the Marina, right after we examined the crime scene. Did you know it was the first time I had proper food in Brighton, that was not a sandwich or takeaway?"

Hildegard smiled.

“Then I am glad I invited you tonight, we might come to a neat full circle.”

“It was also when you first told me about the three aspects of murder. I can see now how Andrew manipulated all of them. But I wonder what was the tip of the thread, the point that it all started to unravel to you.”

“I believe I mentioned this to you already: it was Andrew himself. He was the tip of the thread. All roads led to Andrew - all the information we had came from him. We started to look where he told us to. But I guess I never *not* looked at him as a suspect.”

“I remember you also mentioned something about introducing me to the person who solved the murder of several innocent people to uncover the death of the guy's wife. Am I worth the introduction now?”

Once again, Jill was the one who was quicker and spoke, while glancing curiously at Hildegard.

"You already met this woman."

"Helga told me it was not herself."

"And she was right. It was Felicity."

"*Felicity?*"

I was astonished. Hildegard was grinning.

"You probably didn't connect the dots, but I would be surprised if you haven't heard about her before, probably during your time in the academy: F. Browne - that was her single name - the first black woman to be head detective of the MET police in London. I started as her assistant, and she was damn good! It was a sad day when she left."

"Of course I heard about her! But I never imagined her to be *our* Felicity. I can't believe such a talent and an expert like her is wasted in the corner or the Sussex Police in Brighton."

"It's all about perspective, mate. Felicity decided she had enough, and stepped down to pursue the personal side of her life. Some people don't want the drama and the responsibility, they just want to come in, do their job and leave. For them, what's outside of work matters more. It's a very humble move, to watch things from the side and let others shine. Not an easy thing to do."

I did not have anything to say. I was fascinated by the people I knew, and how sometimes you meet someone extraordinary and you don't even know about it. The legendary F. Browne, I worked with her for days. My colleagues would be impressed, and I couldn't wait to tell them. My thoughts were interrupted by Hildegard.

"Felicity once saw something in me, something even I didn't know I had in myself. And I think it's my turn to make the same move. The reason I invited you over was to offer you a job with me, as an assistant investigator."

I think Hildegard was expecting a 'yes', a 'no', even a 'let me think about it', but she definitely was not expecting what I did: I actually sprayed the wine out of my mouth, in the exact same way it happens in movies and TV shows. I wanted to crawl under the table to hide my embarrassment, but Hildegard and Jill were laughing out loud. Jill held her belly and I could see tears forming around Hildegard's eyes. I did not feel like they were laughing at me, and I was quickly laughing with them. When we finally managed to pull ourselves together, Hildegard spoke.

"I know you have to finish your hours at the Police, but I talked to the commissioner and she's happy for you to split your time between the station and my office. Of course, if you would accept it, that would mean you'll have to set up shop in Brighton, and start living here permanently. And I know this was never part of your plans..."

Jill had a curious look on her face when she looked at me and said the next words.

"Oh, but I think we all know how you feel about that now..."

I guess it was not only Hildegard who already knew me really well.

The End

(for now...)

Acknowledgements

I would like to start with the person who is always by my side, supporting me in everything I do, being my best friend, my partner and my biggest fan: my husband Yogi. He is also the person who had to endure me typing in bed, late at night, while he tried to sleep. Sometimes he would tell me it had been enough, I had given the book too much attention and it was now his turn to get some, but most of the time he was patient and understanding. He also got very close to the solution. Danke schön, Yogi. Ich habe dich lieb!

I would also like to thank my friends who volunteered their time to read this book and answer not one, but two surveys about it, so I could be sure everyone else would enjoy it. Some of them are my friends from the physical world, others are my virtual friends from instagram. They are, in alphabetical order: Aaran Murch, Adi Fallaize-Cunnigham, Alex Ruiz, Ana Luiza Nasr, Andy Ryan, Ben McIlvenna, Bradley Whitfield, Carlos Coutinho,

Cristian Mete-Wade, Emmanuel Valentin, Evan Wilkingson, Evin Rattner, Gareth Phipps-Wiliams, Irina Sazonova, Jack Lord, Jose Miguel Colin, Matt Cotsell, Matteo Aiana, Paul Ryan, Rainer Schmidt, Sara Peralta, Sean Kavanaugh, Steven Rolfe, Wes Irvan and Zach Ebling. I hope I didn't forget anyone. Oh, and my sauna colleague Tony Minion, who did all the work in one of our shifts together, while I edited the final version. Hundreds of hugs and love to all of you, you beautiful bunch!

Thank you to all my other friends, both in the physical and virtual world, and my followers on social media. You are always cheering me up and inspiring me to go further, do stuff, like writing a whodunit! You all make this life amazing, and I love you all!!!

Helga Hildegard was loosely inspired by another powerful and incredible woman I have the pleasure of calling my friend: Carolyn Ansell. When I told her I was basing my main detective on her, she was thrilled, without having any idea where I would take this character. Thank you so so much to Carolyn for graciously accepting to be my inspiration. Now, with Hildegard fully formed, I can only hope I created a person as amazing as her.

Muito obrigado to my cousin Vlad Hinkelmann for introducing me to the wonderful world of Hercule Poirot, when I was still learning how to be a person. Talking about Poirot, I could not finish without mentioning three amazing women authors: Lucia Machado de Almeida, who wrote "O Escaravelho do Diabo", the first whodunit I ever read, back in Brazil, when I was still a kid; and Stella Carr, who wrote the book series "Irmãos Encrenca", which I read as a teenager in Brazil. They both awoke and helped mould my love for mysteries. The third is, of course, Dame Agatha Christie, who created Poirot, undoubtedly my favourite fictional character of all times. I hope I made you three proud.

Finally, thank you for purchasing this book. I publish it on my own, so your support really means a lot to me. I hope you liked this book and I hope you are ready for more, because I already have an idea for another story...

Talk to me: bearhinksch@gmail.com

Printed in Poland
by Amazon Fulfillment
Poland Sp. z o.o., Wrocław

18052088R00151